INFINITY WANDE[

#8

EDITED BY GREY WOLF

SELORNIA

Infinity Wanderers issue 8
Edited by Grey Wolf
Cover Art by Robin Stacey

Fiction, Poetry and Artwork: Copyright remains with original authors

ISBN 9798861684613

INFINITY WANDERERS

ISSUE 8

CONTENTS

Christmas 2023

&

New Year 2024

Special

Death of the Author

Joshua Boers

The time elapsed between "to be", when William Shakespeare punctuated the final line of his greatest play yet, and "not to be", when William Shakespeare's still-smoking body smashed into the wall like a ragdoll, was approximately one second—yet for Harvey, it was enough time to reflect. This was not how he expected his swan song performance to go.

He had been treading the boards—or rather, the carpet—of the Gad Community Playhouse. It had been the final scene of the final act of the final night of performances for *The Tempest, Part Two*. He had been shouting the words of the epilogue loud enough even for the retirees who comprised his sparse audience. Today he was Harvey Hayes, star of stage and a few locally-beloved car dealership commercials, but tomorrow he would be one of them. He was quitting. It was getting too hard to remember his lines…

Then Shakespeare hit the wall.

It was messy. Chunks of mortal coil everywhere.

How had he gotten here? This certainly wasn't the Gad, though when he blinked he could still see the afterimage of the stage lights. It was a small, dark room—a prop room?—filled with the wreckage of furniture, costumes, and assorted junk, and illuminated by a few dozen flaming pieces of paper wafting through the air.

"Hello?" said Harvey.

There was no response, but—faced with the prospect of navigating the spooky dead Shakespeare room alone—Harvey was willing to wait.

Most of the papers either landed among the piles of debris—nearly setting a dozen fires—or were consumed in mid-air. There was a candle on the ground—Harvey had just enough wherewithal to light it before the last page went out.

"Hello?"

No answer. Harvey was alone. He closed his eyes, inhaled for a four count, held for four, and then exhaled for eight. He was, as they said at the Gad, fully grounded in his body. But now it was time to explore the space. He opened his eyes and, after a moment, took a step forward—quietly chanting an old diction exercise to drown out the room's accusatory silence.

"Mmm bah pah, datalana ng gah kah…"

The dead man was sprawled facedown in the opposite corner. Harvey took the short journey step by step, focusing so intently on the body that he almost fell down a ladder—seemingly the room's only exit. But he caught himself, kept calm, and carried on. This was no time to panic.

"MMM BAH PAH, DATALANA NG GAH KAH…"

Harvey arrived. He nudged the body with his foot a few times, but accomplished little more than getting sooty footprints on the man's doublet. He gingerly prodded the man's nearly-decapitated head to the side. Even between the sputtering candlelight and the crushed face he could tell that it was Shakespeare—down to the singed goatee and neck ruffle—and that Shakespeare was absolutely, incontrovertibly dead. This would have been the time to panic if the situation weren't so absurd.

Something stung at Harvey's neck. With a valiant shout of "Who goes there!" (which somewhere along the journey from brain to mouth transformed itself into a meek "I didn't do it!") Harvey spun around and snatched into the air. It was part of a manuscript, half-burned with edges still hot to the touch, but unmistakable in the candlelight. Act 1, Scene 1. *The Tempest, Part Two*.

Suddenly Harvey understood what had happened.

The Tempest, Part Two was Shakespeare's final, most unique, and by far worst play. The gist of it, as much as it could be said to have a gist, was that on the way back to Naples, Prospero and the gang got shipwrecked in England where they met an even more powerful sorcerer than last time: William Shakespeare himself. The show got worse from there: new characters introduced themselves and disappeared at random, dozens of voices fought over the tone, and there were serious third act problems (the problem being that the third act was missing, with the play proceeding immediately from Act Two to Act Four).

But Harvey always had a soft spot for this play for one reason: the final epilogue, which was so heartrendingly beautiful that it made Prospero's epilogue from *The Tempest* look like garbage. In it, Shakespeare gave his final thoughts on the craft of writing: asserting not only the power of art to enshrine someone in memory over time, but the complete mastery of art over time. This is why Harvey selected *The Tempest, Part 2* as his final farewell. Harvey was too late for real stardom. He had recently come across a Facebook meme saying to never give up on your dreams because Alan Rickman didn't get his first movie role until he was 42—a fact that, at Harvey's age, was the opposite of inspiring. But he did hope his final performance would somehow live on. Someday, someone would look at his picture in the lobby, dressed in the iconic Shakespeare costume, and that person would wonder: "Who is that?" And then they would look at the plaque.

Harvey was performing that very scene when it happened. He was blinded by the stage lights, shouting the monologue at the top of his lungs. It was all he could see and hear. The meter thud-THUD-thud-THUDed away at his conscious thoughts, like a mantra, emptying his mind of everything else, until for a moment he *was* Shakespeare, and there was the rush of the Thames, and he could smell the woody-blood smell of the ink, and he was following the scritch-scritch of the pen around the final swoop of the final letter of his final word, and *he would be remembered for this…*

The monologue, too transportive for its own good, had sent Harvey back to the exact time and place where Shakespeare had written it. Unfortunately Shakespeare had already been sitting there. The resultant explosion (probably something to do with tachyons, Harvey reasoned) had immolated the manuscript and blasted Shakespeare into that undiscovered country from whose bourn no traveller returns.

Or had it? As Harvey stood paralyzed by his sudden realization, Shakespeare's mustache—perhaps weakened by the proximity of the candle—fell off his face. Harvey took a closer look at the man he had been shocked to discover was Shakespeare, only to be further shocked by the revelation that he wasn't Shakespeare at all. He was dressed like Shakespeare, but the face was all wrong and the beard was glued on. It was an imposter.

The explanation was clear. In the face of *The Tempest, Part Two*'s evident lack of literary merit, scholars had generally agreed to blame it on someone other than Shakespeare. Francis Bacon, the Earl of Oxford, Christopher Marlowe, the Earl of Derby—each of these figures were held by some professor or another to be the true author. One enduring theory held that "William Shakespeare" was merely a pseudonym for an entire secret society of authors, who each wrote plays in turn and eventually decided to collaborate on one final, disastrous farewell. Harold had never been a Shakespeare truther, but, well, the proof was right there. The dead guy wasn't Shakespeare. Evidently, he had fried Bacon.

Harvey believed in breaking down problems into small, manageable chunks. Sure, his greatest historical hero was a fabrication. Sure, he was guilty of manslaughter by way of overzealous acting. Sure, he had to start a new life in Elizabethan England with nothing for guidance but a theater minor from thirty years ago and the half-remembered plot of *Shakespeare in Love*. But those were problems for tomorrow. Right now, he had to get rid of a body.

Harvey crept down the ladder to take inventory of his surroundings. He recognized a backstage when he saw it (although the Gad, his usual venue, did not have one—you had to hide in the bathrooms) and soon he had navigated his way onto a stage. A real stage, with real wooden boards that creaked with real history. Unless Harvey was mistaken, this was the famous Globe Theater. The Bard of Avon (whoever it was) must have been having a late night. This suited Harvey's purposes perfectly. He remembered there was a trapdoor somewhere. Actors had called it "the hell mouth".

Seemed like a good place to start.

It was dark in the Globe, so Harvey operated mostly by feel, until eventually his splintered hand reached a panel of wood separated from the rest. He pried it open and, glancing downward, jumped back with a shout. Someone was already down there. Someone lying very still.

"Hello?" said Harvey.

There was no response.

"...Good morrow?" said Harvey, hoping against hope that the silence was caused by a language barrier.

It was not.

Harvey psyched himself up for a moment ("MMM! BAH! PAH! DAH! TAH! LAH! NAH! NG! GAH! KAH!"), then got on his belly and held his candle into the yawning hell mouth, trying to get a closer look at the corpse.

It was worse than he thought.

Hell was *crammed* with dead Shakespeares.

But again, they weren't *real* Shakespeares. Harvey knew what to look for this time. Even in the sputtering candlelight the faces didn't look anything like the portraits, and the facial hair on the closest Shakespeare looked like makeup. But why was the understage of the Globe packed with dead Shakespeares?

Harvey had interacted with enough divas at the Gad to sense what must have happened. The scholars were right. These must have been the real authors—Bacon, Marlowe, various earls and lords and whoever—each of them writing under the name "William Shakespeare". Each dressed as the man they had invented. They must have gotten together for one last hurrah—but with this many uncompromising artists in one place, things must have gotten violent—leaving only one of them to finish the play. A play that would now never be finished.

As Harvey dragged another body to the Shakespeare hole, he tried to focus on planning his next move. Maybe he could find the Elizabethan equivalent of a cash register somewhere. And yet, he couldn't stop thinking about the things he had seen. Shakespeare was a lie. *The Tempest, Part Two* would never be written. And Harvey Hayes would die, unremembered, in the seventeenth century. But as the body hit the bard pile with a dull thud, Harvey was shocked into sudden clarity.

Maybe Shakespeare *was* a lie. But he didn't have to be.

Harvey had been practicing being Shakespeare for the past four months. He connected with the role so strongly that Time itself had been fooled. He was here for a reason: to finish the work, to inspire future generations the way he had been inspired, to *be Shakespeare*. And what did it matter that he wasn't the *real* Shakespeare? Wasn't the dead poet society under the floorboards proof enough that it was the *idea* of Shakespeare that really mattered? This was the second chance Harvey never thought he would get, and he would be a fool not to take it.

Harvey returned to the prop room and set himself up a writing desk from what little unbroken furniture remained. He was William Shakespeare, his greatest role yet, and now it was time to write Shakespeare's greatest play. Maybe he would give himself a little cameo—nothing too big, just enough for people to remember his name. Harvey would feel smug about that until the day he died.

Now if he could only remember how it went…

#

The Tempest, Part Two was nearly finished and Harvey had done a pretty good job. He was a little fuzzy on his lines, and the scenes where he hadn't personally been onstage were a total blur, but he made some educated guesses about the plot and worked from there. He had even punched it up a little—added some jokes, some new characters, put the ol' Harvey spin on everything. It came together, kind of.

But there was one part of the show Harvey remembered with perfect clarity and didn't dare touch. The final epilogue—the one that had caused all this trouble. He knew someday it would inspire someone the way it had inspired him. For a second, that person would *be* Shakespeare—and they would hear the rush of the Thames, and smell the woody-blood smell of the ink, and follow the scritch-scritch of the pen around the final swoop of the final letter of his final word…

Harvey finally put it all together.

It's a cycle! Every time this play is written, another actor gets transported back in time, blows up the previous actor, and rewrites the play from memory! That's why there are so many dead Shakespeares lying around! They aren't 16th century authors at all – they're from the future, like me!

The full weight of this discovery hit Harvey as he was punctuating the final word of his play, but it was too late to stop the motion of his own hand.

The time elapsed between "to be", when Harvey Hayes punctuated the final line of his greatest play yet, and "not to be", when Harvey Hayes' still-smoking body smashed into the wall like a ragdoll, was approximately one second…

Joshua Boers

Joshua Boers lives in Grand Rapids, Michigan. When he isn't writing, he can generally be found browsing used bookstores, playing with his cat Mishka, or falling asleep to episodes of Frasier. By day, he is an assistant editor at an independent book publisher.

Twitter: **twitter.com/JoshuaBoers**

Instagram: **instagram.com/joshuaboers**

Author Interview

Gary Beck

Gary Beck has spent most of his adult life as a theater director and worked as an art dealer when he couldn't earn a living in the theater. He has also been a tennis pro, a ditch digger and a salvage diver. His original plays and translations of Moliere, Aristophanes and Sophocles have been produced Off Broadway. His poetry, fiction and essays have appeared in hundreds of literary magazines and his published books include 39 poetry collections, 14 novels, 4 short story collections, 2 collection of essays and 8 books of plays. Gary lives in New York City.

1) **How long have you been writing?** I started writing poetry at the age of 16, imitations of the British romantics, Byron, Keats, Shelley. I learned about rhyme, meter and great poetry, but it wasn't what I wanted to write. That was a long time ago. Then I started discovering my own poetic voice, wrote short stories and plays. When my theater closed in 1996 I had time to write novels, essays, short stories and a lot more poetry.

2) **What is the earliest work of yours that you have published or intend to publish?** My first book, Expectations, a poetry collection, was published in 2010. I had individual poems published in literary magazines as early as the 1960s.

3) **Who were the earliest authors to be an inspiration for your writing? Which other authors do you consider to be an inspiration and for what reason?** The earliest author who inspired me was Walt Whitman. His great compassion serving as a nurse in the Civil War revealed the scope of his true character. My favorite saying comes from him 'Resist much. Obey little.' The next author was John Steinbeck, particularly In Dubious Battle and The Grapes of Wrath. He recognized the greed of capitalism and wrote about it from the viewpoint of the poor and oppressed, who never quit fighting for a better life.

4) **Which was the first book you published?** The first book of mine that was published was Expectations, my first poetry collection. It was published by a good medium size house that promised publicity and promotion, readings and other efforts to get the book known. They went out of business the day the book was released – sic transit gloria mundi.

5) **Other than authors, who are your heroes?** My first hero was John L. Lewis, president of the Coal Miner Union in the 1940s and 50s. He worked for the benefit of the workers, coal mining one of dangerous jobs there is, fighting the bosses for fair wages and treatment. My most recent hero is former Congresswoman Liz Cheney, the only person of courage to resist Donald Trump, which cost her the elected office and her public voice.

6) **If you could go back in time to learn the truth about one historical mystery or disputed event, what would it be?** I would go back to February 15, 1898, to the sinking of the Maine in Havana Harbor, which launched the Spanish American War. It was never determined who or what caused the explosion that sank the ship and provoked war.

7) **Do you have any names or surnames that tend to crop up and repeat themselves throughout your stories, without the intention being there to make them related in any way? How have your life experiences informed your writing?** Every once in a while, I discovered after the fact that I used a name that I used before, within a play, novel, or short story. I don't know whether it's coincidence, Freudian reenactment, or carelessness.

8) **Other Questions** In one way or another, all my life experiences influenced my writing. The most profound influence was working with disadvantaged youth in prisons and public housing, then homeless families with children. The poverty and suffering of innocent youth who did not cause their condition is a crime against humanity.

9) **How did you get into the performance of, and later the translation of, ancient Greek plays?** I was a theatre director for most of my adult life, but never did the classics. I started my own theatre company in 1976 with a 10 year plan to do the classics. I started with Commedia del' Arte, inspired by scenarios of the IGelosi, the first professional theatre company. The next cycle was 4 plays by Moliere that I translated and directed. Then I translated and directed 3 plays by Aristophanes and Lysistrata was our first hit show. I was preparing to take it to a legitimate 299 seat Off Broadway theatre when I lost my theatre and a major government grant. After that it was more complicated to produce the classics, but I translated and directed 3 plays by Sophocles, then translated and directed Aeschylus Agamemnon, the last classic I did.

10) What are your plans for the future? My future plans are to continue writing poetry books and novels as long as I can. I do occasional poetry readings and play readings with actors from my former company. Everything else is fortuitous.

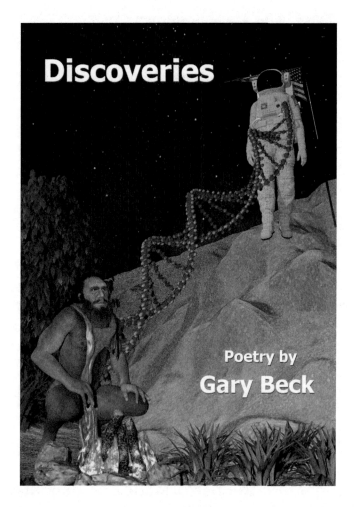

Gary's new poetry collection, Discoveries, is available in paperback, and will shortly be available in kindle and other ebook formats.

http://purpleunicornmedia.com/discoveries.html

For The Children Taken By The Pied Piper

Jack Cariad Leon

The following is a poem from a version of history where the children taken by the Pied Piper were returned at some point. It's a situation that always puzzled and intrigued me, but I also really wondered for how the mothers of those children must have felt. I wanted to create a happy vision.

Saturn's rings had lit up on the night that you
were all seamlessly, quietly taken;
it sensed a tragedy on our small planet of blue
and it was nothing we were faking.

When you all collectively came back
your complexions were all so wan, so pale, your
fingers were stained formless black.
Felt frozen, no matter how hot a bath we'd pour.

The messages meant for you,
will eventually find their way through.
Just remember to keep those *minds*
open as those *ears* and *eyes*.

It could be redirected many times
but you'll always have those little signs
and although it's true time was wasted,
I know you all will find your places.

I understand breakfast may be all that you can take

for now as you prepare to rejoin civilisation

before you require recovery for the rest of the day.

Soon you can work on your own recreation.

And so I decided that I need for you all to know,

that if I ever choose to string you along

it'll be with ribbons of light and love, never woe

and that's why I wrote you all this song.

Jack Cariad Leon

Jack Cariad Leon (he/him) is a transgender writer and visual artist based in Brisbane, Australia. A fan of the avant-garde, he collects dolls and art books of certain genres. He also has a deep interest in the history and lore of flowers.

Small Causes 7 - History-Changing Events

L.G. Parker

Small Causes

In his treatise, *Bellum Gallicum,* no less a history maker than Julius Caesar observed, "In Bello Parvis Momentis Magni Casus Intercedunt." (In war great events are the results of small causes.) Caesar had the truth of it. Relatively minor actions, snap decisions, capricious weather and other random events can change the course of battle. Relatively minor battles can change the course of wars. Relatively minor wars can change the course of history. For example muddy fields led to French disasters at Agincourt and Waterloo leading to the rise of England and the downfall of Napoleon. Italy's intervention in Albania brought the vainglorious Mussolini into proximity with Greece. As a neutral nation Greece was no threat to the Axis; indeed it served as a strategic buffer state but Mussolini could not control his appetite for empire. Jealous of the military success of his fascist ally he launched an ill advised invasion of Hellas. When the Italian army failed and a Greek counter-offensive drove deep into Albania, German resources were required to rectify the situation and protect the oil fields of Ploesti. The campaigns in Yugoslavia and Greece to secure the Axis Southern flank delayed the initial battles of Operation Barbarossa for five weeks. The loss of precious time, wear and tear on men and equipment, poor operational decisions by the Führer and the early onset of a historically brutal winter, doomed Barbarossa. Hitler's panzers arrived at the outskirts of Moscow in December 1941 rather than October or November; too little, too late. Stymied in Russia and now at war with the United States the strategic balance of power in Europe had drastically changed.

Two years prior to the events in Greece a small, relatively unknown battle on the border of Mongolia and Russia in 1939 determined the course of World War II in the Pacific. Soundly defeated by a rising military star, Georgi Zhukov, Japan fatally altered its strategic war plans. Initially remarkably victorious, a vicious fight in the jungles of New Guinea determined the limits of the Japanese advance in the South Pacific just as a mismatched fleet action between the Imperial Japanese Navy (IJN) and the United States Navy (USN) not only determined the limits of their advance in the central Pacific but also reversed the balance of power between Japan and America. The Battle for Okinawa, the largest invasion in the history of modern warfare and the final battle of the Pacific war, influenced far more than the immediate conflict. It sent ripples through time that affected the fifty year Cold War that followed. This series of historical articles will examine the ***Small Causes*** of battles, events and people both great and not so great that shaped the course of history as we know it. They are a treasure trove of "what if" scenarios that serve as a reminder of the fragility of that edifice we call history.

Part VII

History Changing Events

INTRODUCTION:

The chronicle of mankind is replete with history changing events upon which the fate of millions rest. Even relatively unknown battles can have consequences that extend far beyond their immediate aftermath; results that alter the world for centuries to come; effects that continue to impact national and international dynamics long after the details of the event have been all but forgotten.

For example, a wrong turn by his driver brought Arch Duke Franz Ferdinand into contact with Gavrilo Princip. His assassination precipitated World War I. A chance arrow to the eye ended the life of King Harold II and brought Norman rule to England. A stray bullet took the life of General Albert Sidney Johnston. His death removed the South's most effective general from the Western Theatre of the Confederacy. Such is the fine line between history as we know it and history as it might have been. What follows is a short review of crucial historic events where something as simple as a search for new shoes for an army forever changed history. Consider the possibilities had things gone just a bit differently and what the world would look like now.

******

On 18 April 1943 a squadron of United States Army Air Force (USAAF) Lockheed P-38 Lightning's intercepted and shot down a Japanese Mitsubishi G4M bomber (Allied designation Betty) escorted by six Mitsubishi A6M Zeroes. On this particular mission the Betty was not loaded with ordnance but was transporting Admiral Yamamoto from Rabaul to Bougainville. After the Japanese defeat on Guadalcanal Yamamoto thought it important to tour the front lines to rally the troops. American code breakers had deciphered the message traffic pertaining to this inspection tour however. Armed with the specifics of the tour to include dates, locations, arrival and departure times an ambush was planned utilizing the long range American P-38 fighter. A Japanese patrol found the wreckage and located Yamamoto's body the following day. The story may have been embellished to preserve his reputation but according to the report Yamamoto had been thrown from the plane and was seated under a tree clutching his ceremonial Katana in a white gloved hand. Fortunately for the Allies and unfortunately for the Japanese Yamamoto's most likely successor, the brilliant Rear Admiral Yamaguchi, had gone down with the carrier *Hiryu* at Midway the year before.

* * * * * *

Born and raised in Kansas Dwight David Eisenhower dreamed of the ocean and had his dreams come true he would have made his career in the Navy. When it came time to matriculate his first choice was the Naval Academy. West Point was an afterthought. On the entrance exams he placed first for Annapolis and second for the Military Academy. By the time everything had been processed however Eisenhower was too old to enter the Navy. His disappointment was short lived for soon thereafter the number one candidate for West Point dropped out. Eisenhower promptly accepted his spot. The rest, as they say, is history but consider this. Many debate Eisenhower's strategic and tactical ability but nearly everyone agrees that very few, if any, of the senior American Officers available in 1941 could have held together the often contentious, even rancorous alliance or dealt with the monumental egos of Montgomery and Patton much less Roosevelt and Churchill. That took discipline, self-control, tact and political acumen which Eisenhower possessed in abundance. Many of his contemporaries were suspicious of the English if not outright Anglophobes. Few possessed his extensive staff experience or his organizational talent. An Admiral Eisenhower would have greatly weakened, if not completely jeopardized the alliance.

* * * * * *

In 1947 a young baseball player named Fidel Castro tried out for a spot with the Washington Senators. Unfortunately for the United States, Cuba and the world at large Castro did not make the team. In his alternative profession Castro would reduce his once prosperous country to abject poverty, drive thousands into exile, dispatch Cuban mercenaries to South America and Africa fomenting revolution, sowing the seeds of endless misery, poverty and strife in those regions that continue to this day and bring the world to the brink of nuclear war when the United States and the Soviet Union squared off during the Cuban Missile Crisis.

* * * * * *

Another young man, Adolf Hitler, dreamed of becoming either an artist or an architect. He applied twice to the Academy of Fine Arts in Vienna and was twice rejected. The Academy's Dean thought Hitler displayed an aptitude for architecture however and recommended him to that department. A high school diploma, which Hitler did not have, was required to enter the School of Architecture. To the detriment of the entire world the school declined to waive the requirement.

* * * * * *

It is well known that President Lincoln was assassinated at Ford's Theatre in April 1865. Less well known is the fact that General Grant and his wife were to have been guests of the Lincoln's that evening but declined earlier the same day. Had Grant not chosen to board a train to visit his children in New Jersey the United States might have lost not only the current President but also a future President.

* * * * * *

A Persian victory at Salamis or Plataea and the world never knows Aristotle, Euclid, Plato or Socrates - in short Western Civilization ends before it begins. In due course Imperial Rome absorbs Greek culture and spreads its influence throughout the Western world. For a thousand years after the fall of Rome the Byzantine Empire holds at bay the barbarian hordes of the East ensuring the traditions of Greece and Rome survive long enough to take root and thrive in the West. Without the political acumen of Justinian, the organizational skills of Narses and the military genius of Belisarius Byzantium might have imploded during the Nika Rebellion of 532. Instead of falling into civil war the Eastern Roman Empire thrives. The Byzantines reconquer North Africa and Italy, Justinian codifies Roman law which spreads throughout the realm greatly influencing the legal systems that follow. In short Constantinople becomes the repository of western culture and holds that ancient learning in safekeeping until its fall in 1453.

* * * * * *

An arrow to the eye of Harold II turned the tide of battle at Hastings (14 October 1066) resulting in the Norman conquest of England. William II became King of England as well as Duke of Normandy. From that point forward English Kings could claim hereditary lands and titles in France. French monarchs considered their English counterparts vassals and could and did demand oaths of fealty and proper homage. Thus the stage was set for centuries of conflict between the two emerging nations. Arrows (and heavy rain the night before) again played a decisive role at Agincourt (25 October 1415) when the common yeoman archer armed with his powerful English longbow slaughtered the flower of French nobility.

* * * * * *

The defeat of the Spanish Armada in 1588, due more to gales and poor Iberian seamanship than British naval skill, ensured that England would retain its sovereignty, remain Protestant rather than be forcibly returned to the Catholic church, become a maritime power and eventually supplant the Dutch, French and Spanish as the dominant colonial power. This amalgam of Celts, Vikings, Romans and Franks forged on the anvil of war produced the uniquely English culture that found its way to the New World and grew into America.

* * * * * *

In 9A.D. the XVII, XVIII and XIX Legions commanded by Quintilius Varus were led into an ambush by a Germanic Chieftain called Arminius. Varus thought Arminius loyal to Rome and accepted his offer to lead the Romans against his countrymen. In fact Arminius harbored bitter resentment toward the Empire and had forged a coalition of like minded tribes to oppose Rome's incursions beyond the Rhine. Against the advice of his senior officers Varus followed Arminius through the Teutoburger Wald. There on a narrow neck of land between the dense forest and a near impassable marsh the Germans struck. Caught in a long column of march the Romans were unable to form defensive squares. With the column broken in several places, fighting degenerated into separate mêlées. Under the circumstances Roman tactics, usually dominant on any battlefield, could not prevail against German numbers and the battle became a slaughter. The loss of three legions plus auxiliaries ensured the Roman frontier in Gaul remained the Rhine rather than the Elbe. Italy, France, Spain and England were profoundly influenced by centuries of Latin domination. Northwest Europe, for better or for worse, was shaped by the Germanic tribes.

* * * * * *

In 636A.D. the forces of the once powerful Byzantines, now known as the Eastern Roman Empire, a domain in eclipse, met the armies of Khalid Ibn al Walid at Yarmuk. A victory by the Byzantines might very well destroy the nascent religion which had stormed out of the desert just four years after the death of Mohamed or, at the very least, confine it to the Arabian Peninsula from which it had sprung. As fate would have it the Muslims won a decisive victory paving the way for the expansion of Islam throughout the Middle East, Anatolia and Egypt. Over the next one hundred years the word and the sword would carry the banners of Islam through North Africa and into Spain. In 1453 Constantinople fell; Greece, Macedonia and the Balkans followed. By 1529 Vienna itself was under siege. At the time the Islamic juggernaut seemed unstoppable and but for a handful of critical battles Western Civilization would have died in its infancy.

* * * * * *

At the Battle of Tours also known as Poitiers (732) Charles Martel routed the forces of Abd ar Rahman earning his sobriquet 'The Hammer' but more importantly his victory checked the Arab advance into Western Europe thereby preserving its Roman heritage. Latin culture formed the foundation of the Carolingian Empire forged by his son Pippin III and grandson Charlemagne that would evolve over the centuries into modern France. The Muslims or Moors as they were known continued to hold Spain but would eventually be driven into North Africa during the Reconquista.

* * * * * *

Selim the Sot, contrary to the Koran's prohibitions, had a fondness for Cypriot wine and to ensure ample stocks of the vintage for his table, captured the island in 1570. The reaction in the west was unprecedented. The Holy League of Venice, the Habsburg dominions, Malta, Genoa and other Italian City States stopped feuding among themselves long enough to assemble a fleet of 210 galleys and fregatas armed with cannon. In 1571, off the western coast of Greece near Lepanto (Navpaktos) on the Gulf of Patras, the Allied fleet commanded by Don Juan of Austria clashed with 275 Turkish galleys. The Ottoman Turks, who still favored the ancient naval tactic of ramming and boarding, were no match for the well protected and well armed Christian fleet. In the battle that followed Don Juan destroyed or captured over 200 Turkish galleys at a cost of just fifteen of the Holy League's vessels. The near total destruction of the Ottoman fleet, its first defeat in over two centuries, resounded through the East and the West. Although Barbary Pirates would continue to plague the Mediterranean for centuries to come, the major naval threat had been removed allowing Western commerce to flourish.

* * * * * *

Lepanto was not the first naval battle between Christians and Muslims. Equally important but much less well known was the engagement that took place in 1509 on the Indian Ocean near the port of Diu. 1500 years after the birth of Christ, Christianity was largely confined to Europe and Western Europe was a dark, stagnant, semi-barbaric land living in the shadow of the glory that had been ancient Rome. In half that time Islam had spread from Arabia west into Spain, east as far as the Philippines, north to the gates of Vienna and south along the coast of Africa. In contrast to an impoverished feudal Europe where learning had all but vanished and as for the fine arts only the art of war flourished, the Caliphate was an enlightened, thriving empire made enormously rich by its trade with China, Indonesia and India. The Mamluks ruled in Egypt, their rivals, the Ottomans, in Anatolia.

Ironically it was the crusades that brought about a renaissance in Europe. Contact with the Byzantine or Eastern Roman Empire rekindled the lamp of learning in the west; trade with the Muslims (1) sparked a desire for the riches of the Far East; both worked in conjunction to foster the spirit of exploration. As the general level of education improved technology improved and as technology improved ships and seamanship improved and the European explorers pushed further and further. In addition to castles feudal lords began to erect universities and great cathedrals. Cathedrals required some means to summon the faithful. Guilds arose to provide massive bronze bells. From the casting of bells it was but a short step to the casting of large caliber cannon.

With England and France embroiled in near continuous dynastic wars Spain, Portugal and the Netherlands enjoyed a period of supremacy. Since the Venetians, Genoese and Turks controlled the Mediterranean daring Portuguese merchants seeking to eliminate the Muslim middleman and gain direct access to the wealth of the Far East pushed around the Cape of Good Hope into the Indian Ocean and thus into the maritime source of Muslim wealth. Determined to rid Islam of this Christian threat the Mamluks persuaded the Ottomans to aid them. Between the two great powers the Muslims assembled a fleet of 200 galleys. Near Diu the Portuguese met the enemy with just seventeen vessels. Comrade Stalin famously noted, "Quantity has a quality all its own." In this case however the Portuguese ships were so far superior numbers could not prevail. Much larger with numerous cannon in broadside the Portuguese ships made short work of the Muslim galleys ill suited as they were for open ocean warfare. Its navy destroyed the Mamluks could not protect their merchant fleet which gradually disappeared from the Indian Ocean. The loss of trade so weakened the Mamluks that they fell victim to their one time allies the Ottomans eight years later. What the Mamluks lost the Portuguese gained and for a time they were a power to be reckoned with. Eventually they succumbed to the Dutch who in turn gave way to the French and English.

* * * * * *

In 1683 the Ottoman Turks again laid siege to Vienna. At the direction of Sultan Mehmed IV, his Grand Vizier, Kara Mustafa Pasha, invested the city. The Grand Vizier took defensive measures to prevent any rescue attempt but did not go so far as to build lines of contravallation thinking the city would fall to his army estimated at 90,000 long before any relief forces could be organized and arrive. Pope Innocent XI called upon the faithful to aid Count Ernst Rudiger von Starhemberg and the 16,000 defenders of the beleaguered city. Duke Charles of Lorraine, Maximilian II Emanuel of Bavaria, Johann Georg III of Saxony and Jan III Sobieski of Poland answered the Papal summons. At the Battle of Kahlenberg the allied forces of the Holy League broke into the Ottoman camp and in the panic that followed routed the Turkish forces. In the aftermath Kara Mustafa was executed, Sultan Mehmed IV deposed and more importantly Vienna relieved. By 1699 Ottoman forces had been driven out of all of Hungary. Over the next two centuries the Ottomans would be driven back into Anatolia and Greece and the immensely troubled and troublesome Balkan states would achieve independence.

* * * * * *

On 05 September 1781 the French West Indies Fleet did something extremely rare in the annals of history - they soundly defeated a British fleet off the Virginia Capes sealing the fate of the Army besieged at Yorktown. Cut off from supply and with no means of escape Cornwallis was forced to surrender on 19 October 1781, another rarity in British history up until that time. This defeat brought about the fall of Lord North's cabinet in March 1782. The Marquis of Rockingham formed a new government pledged to negotiations with the Americans. On 12 April 1782 the British destroyed the French West Indies fleet in a naval battle off Iles des Saintes. Had that engagement occurred six months earlier the outcome of the Revolutionary War is much less certain for the British still held the major cities of New York, Charleston and Savannah. The conflict might have dragged on, then again, the colonies were at the end of their economic tether and morale had plummeted among soldiers and civilians alike.

CONCLUSION:

General history textbooks organize history into eras such as the Renaissance, the Reformation and the Industrial Revolution. This thematic presentation has its place however the trillions of small events that comprise these epic movements are lost in this type of approach. Also lost are the consequences of these small events. For example, when Napoleon formed the Confederation of the Rhine or Rheinbund his primary motive was to establish a buffer zone between Prussia, Austria and France. His ulterior motive was to reward his family, generals and other supporters with land and titles. This act reduced approximately three hundred small duchies, ecclesiastical cities, electorates and principalities to just three dozen states. Napoleon could not have foreseen that these thirty odd states would unite at the machinations of Otto von Bismarck in 1871 and bedevil France in 1914 and again in 1941. Also lost in this broad brush rendering of history are many of the more intriguing events and their connections to later events that would otherwise remain mere footnotes to history. For example, small gunboats played a critical part in the decisive British victory at Omdurman during the Mahdist War. Commanding the gunboat **Fateh** was Lieutenant David Richard Beatty. Also present at Omdurman was none other than an adventurous youngster named Winston Churchill serving with the 4TH Hussars. Beatty would rise through the ranks (thanks in no small part to his acquaintance with Churchill formed during that campaign) to become Admiral of the Fleet, Earl Beatty and First Sea Lord. In command of the 1ST Battlecruiser Squadron at the Battle of Jutland he famously remarked, "There seems to be something wrong with our bloody ships today." Jutland was a strategic victory for the British but a tactical victory for the Germans. One of the bloody ships lost to the German High Seas Fleet at Jutland was HMS *Invincible*. *Invincible* was the flagship of Admiral Sir Horace Lambert Alexander Hood another veteran of Omdurman where as a Lieutenant he commanded the gunboat *Nasir.* A shell from SMS *Derfflinger* breached *Invincible's* "Q" turret and penetrated her magazine resulting in a catastrophic explosion that blew the ship in half. Of her crew of 1021 only six survived. Admiral Hood went down with his ship. In similar fashion his namesake HMS *Hood* would fall victim to the *Bismarck* twenty-five years later. Such are the small events and their connections to later events that make history so fascinating. Equally fascinating is the realization if you were to break that connection at any point in the chain of events history becomes quite different. Therein lies the interesting realm of alternate history.

ENDNOTES:

(1) When the Christians and Muslims were not killing one another they were trading and European lust for the pearls of Persia, the gold of India, the silks of China and the spices of Indonesia made the land of Islam fabulously wealthy, in effect funding the very armies they were fighting. In the same manner today, when we purchase oil from the Middle East we fund the very people who have vowed to destroy Western Civilization proof, if you needed any, that we never learn anything from history.

Slender Threads by L.G. Parker

History is an intricately woven tapestry hanging in space and time. Remove one thread, replace it with another, and the entire picture changes.

Slender Threads by L G Parker includes One Stay Bullet - a different Battle of Shiloh and The Story Behind One Stray Bullet, including subsequent what-ifs, and how the battle defined the lives and future direction of such as Lew Wallace, James Garfield, Henry Morton Stanley and George Erasmus Dixon, inventor of the submersible CSS Hunley.

What if Winston Churchill had died at the Battle of Omdurman in 1898, or after being knocked down in the street in New York in 1931? Slender Threads looks in detail at subjects such as Lee's Triumph in an alternate history of the Battle of Evelington Heights during the American Civil War, or the Leyte Gulf plans of the Imperial Japanese Navy in World War Two.

https://www.amazon.co.uk/dp/1910718300

L. G. Parker

L. G. Parker is a retired Naval Surface Warfare Officer and Senior Naval Science Instructor with a lifelong interest in Science Fiction and history; especially the "What If" scenarios where Science Fiction and History merge; that intriguing place where events balance precariously on the fulcrum of human interaction and the smallest details can tip the outcome of those events one way or another; the fascinating realm of alternate history. When he is not reading, researching and writing he spends his days kayaking and hiking to waterfalls in the Great Smoky Mountains of North Carolina with his wife of forty-seven years.

More of his work can be found at:

https://fromsmallcausesgreatevents.org

https://WH40KMalleusMaleficarum.com

Mol's Swansong

Susan Dean

Mol was lounging seductively against the bar one tightly laced booted foot resting on the brass foot rail her skirts hoisted to just above the knee revealing a stocking held cheekily in place by a lace garter. Her right arm rested casually on the bar the grimy white linen of the puff sleeve of her low cut bodice slipping tantalisingly from her bare shoulder. She was laughing and joking with customers of The Old Bee Hive Inn and had just succeeded in procuring a flagon of ale from one when Harry, the landlord walked in 'haway now Mol, watch they sen I've heard tell The Queen Anne's Revenge was seen docking. Best watch thy sen Edward divvina like you messin' with the customers.' 'Alreet Harry, lass as her job to do divvin she?' 'Aye, lass but Edward divvina see it that way he catches you it'll put him in a right fettle aye.' Mol sighed playfully pinched the cheek of the customer who had bought the ale, winked and left her position at the bar then with a tantalising sway of her hips looked back and huskily said 'later pet next door, upstairs The Quilted Camel.'

The Old Bee Hive and The Quilted Camel were adjoining inns the former reputed to be the oldest in Newcastle positioned on the quayside at the base of Sandhill overlooking Gateshead.

Edward Robinson had been born in The Old Bee Hive and it was still his favourite haunt whenever The Queen Anne's Revenge was in port now that piracy enjoyed legal status at least for the present. Robinson had joined Blackbeard in his youth and was now one of his most trusted men and he didn't like anyone messing with Mol despite being a prostitute he regarding her as his property, his wor lass.

Mol was out back tidying herself up when Edward walked in 'Edward, I mean Mr Robinson' Harry fussed looking a little nervous Robinson brushed past him 'clamming for me bait, Harry' Robinson curtly replied setting his amble frame down on a wrought iron chair in front of a matching table with a well scrubbed wooden top. 'Where's wor lass, Harry?' the landlord swallowed 'she's, she's out back Edward, I mean Mr Robinson, sir that is' 'aye gan fetch her then her wor lad's hyem' 'whey aye' stammered Harry and scuttled off sighing with relief producing a grimy handkerchief to mop his sweating brow.

'Edward' exclaimed Mol appearing through the dark cave like rear entrance placing her left arm across his broad shoulders feeling muscles rippling beneath his clothing. Edward made a grasp for her swinging her down onto his lap Mol place both arms around his neck 'Edward canny to see thee again' Edward planted a kiss on her cheek while fumbling in his coat pocket then shouted over his shoulder 'Harry me scram' 'Mol a luv ye pet divvin I always bring ye a bauble from me booty aye?' 'aye ye do Edward' 'well how da ye like that then' placing a gold plated silver spangle in her outstretched palm 'now there's a pretty thing' she smiled holding it up to the light where it gleamed 'aye well put it on then.' Harry appeared placed a flagon of ale and a plate of pie and mash on the table and disappeared as quickly as he had appeared, Edward kept Mol on his lap while he ate.

As the afternoon progressed towards evening Edward got drunker and the more he drank the more unpleasant he became then through blurring vision he noticed something he didn't like at all. Mol had long since slipped from his grasp and was roaming among the customers clearly showing off her charms and the bauble. Then he noticed one customer in particular paying more attention than he liked and his anger began rising but when he noticed Mol candle in hand entice a customer towards the rear of the bar and that dark cavernous entrance where the shared privy with The Quilted Camel was along with a dark cobbled passageway leading to the inn next door where Mol had a room upstairs. His temper boiled over he lurched drunkenly up staggering in a gan propa radge after the couple roaring 'you slut I'll stop you harlot' as he made a lunge for the back entrance.

The bar fell silent all eyes fixed on the cave-like exit and the raised voices beyond it 'alreet, ye can have thee lass' one voice shouted 'aye, I'll have the lass I'll teach her to cuckold me. That's wor lass leave her be' 'wor lass' scoffed the first voice 'can ye no see what sort of lass she is' a crack was heard as Edward broke the man's nose then a full scale fight broke out and in the ensuing mayhem both men forgot Mol who caught in the middle was desperately trying to get away while trying to hold on to the candle.

But a sudden blood curdling scream brought both men back to their senses the candle Mol had been holding had been knocked from her hand but as it fell before extinguishing itself had caught the frill around the hem of Mol's bodice which attached it to her skirt at the waist and Mol went up in flames her piercing screams quickly replaced by the smell of roasting flesh.

The bar was so shocked that both men had made a frantic run for it through the bar of The Quilted Camel and out into the night before anyone knew what was happening. Six months later The Queen Anne's Revenge sank of the coast off North Carolina, some say by Blackbeard himself, thereby leaving only dead men who tell no tales.

Poetry

Linda M. Crate

his sun, her moon

the princess
didn't feel
as if she
belonged,

always she was
compared to her
superior sisters;

one day she
decided she'd had
enough of high society—

she rescued a dragon
her brother was meant to
slay, and they flew off
into a sunset never to be
seen again;

and she found a prince
who didn't mind
how eccentric she was—

they were wed,
and she lived happily
ever after,
without having to swallow
herself down;
free to be who she was
every day and there were no
comparisons to be made

for she was his sun
and he was her moon.

-linda m. crate

never needed you less

if you wanted to run
around in the
forest of your darkness
alone then you shouldn't
have tried to drag
me into your trees,

you could've stayed alone
if all you were going to do
was break me in the teeth
of your lust;

if it were up to me
a werewolf would lose his fangs—

but i am content i no longer
love you,
because you never loved me;

only wanted my body
not my soul—

when i looked in the mirror
after you married the woman
you cheated on me with i saw
a monster,

it took me a while to understand
that you were the monster;

i was just the collateral damage

standing in the wake
of your nightmares—

took me many moons to
remember how to put the stars
back in my eye, but i have;
and i never needed you less.

-linda m. crate

cut to pieces by your lust

i think the butterfly
was telling me
to run away,

fancied you to be
some sort of

loyal werewolf who'd
sweep me off my feet;
who'd always lend me
light when my mind brought
me to darkness

instead you buried me—

but what is soil to
a vampire?

i shook off the shock,
the anger, the pain,
and the betrayal;

fought tooth and nail to get
out of that cold and dark
earth
popping up like a sunflower
i launched myself at
my mother the moon

knowing she'd heal all my wounds
& she did—

lust isn't love,
that was a lesson i had
to learn the hard way;
for while i loved you
there's only one thing you wanted
of me and you took my flowers
leaving me stranded in the limbo of darkness
cut to pieces by your lust.

-linda m. crate

the dragon and the faerie

they wanted to control her,
and they told her to be
meek and humble;
someone they could make
crumble under the pressure
of their demands—

but she resisted,
persisted
without them in her life;

she was wild and fierce

and the dragon born prince
made her his bride

for he was wild and fierce, too—

together the faerie princess
and the dragon prince found a
love so deep that no ocean
could bury it,
and a love so full that even a
sip never seemed like enough
for either of them.

-linda m. crate

the peony queen

a queen with hair
of peonies,
they already whispered
behind their hands
saying she was cursed;

but her wife loved her
regardless of their words—

the peony queen was
kind but shy,
but her wife was outspoken
enough for the both of them;

they insisted she was dangerous
but the wife said that she was
the vampire so the only thing they
ought to fear was her losing her
temper for making a mockery of
her wife—

they didn't listen,
and killed her petal;

so she destroyed every last one
for she could not endure the thought
of monsters destroying the most
beautiful person she had ever known
without being punished for the crime—

she then walked into the sunlight,
asking the universe for another
chance for romance in the next life;

a life where she and her petal could bloom.

-linda m. crate

wild pixie

they tried to destroy her,
but she was magic;

in one life she was a mermaid,
the next a vampire,
after that a werewolf,
she was an elf,
and a faerie, too;

in this life she was a pixie

and she was wild as ever
because even as an immortal
life was never promised
forever—

she wanted a life where she lived,

and all they wanted to do
was tame and dull her fierce spirit;
but they found the more they tried to
squash her—

their cages only were destroyed
and devoured by the earth,

she would never be their toy.

-linda m. crate

Linda M. Crate

Linda M. Crate (she/her) is a Pennsylvanian writer whose poetry, short stories, articles, and reviews have been published in a myriad of magazines both online and in print. She has twelve published chapbooks the latest being: Searching Stained Glass Windows For An Answer (Alien Buddha Publishing, December 2022). She is also the author of the novella Mates (Alien Buddha Publishing, March 2022). Her debut book of photography Songs of the Creek (Alien Buddha Publishing, April 2023) was recently published.

And Lilith Sewed The Seam

Allister Nelson

The frost came early that year, the year the Queen of Night came to Karelia. We lived in Sharon, a little shtetl in Grand Russe on the Finnish border that was known for its beautiful alpine aerials and lakes like beads of blue glass. The ocean, too, was refreshing to swim in – provided one went to the banya afterwards. I was a young lass in the rime-laden harbors and forests of Sharon. We Jews of Sharon were a sailing, seabound lot, making our living off fishing and the waves. But mama, bubbe and I? We were seamstresses of the finest caliber. Some would say we were magick. They called us, and our shop, The Weaving Wives.

The boyars ordered traditional kaftans straight from bubbe's shop, woven with the earth goddess Mokosh and her lovers Veles and Perun on the breast. But I had grown up toeing the line between two faiths, both the myths of Baba Yaga eating unworthy children and the Night Howler Agrath screech-dancing on the roof to mark a house that her husband, Sammael, would strike down as dogs bayed at his twelve-winged flight. Sometimes, late at night, I could hear them.

Or perhaps it was only a storm…

Words of bubbe's and mama's and my craftiness spread, and soon, the tsarina herself ordered a cape from us that was all the rage, the year I turned sixteen. It was based off the tale of Father Frost's granddaughter, Snegurochka the Snow Maiden. A tale I had always loved. It was the first project I was given complete ownership of.

I embroidered white, pale pink and dove gray pearls on the powder blue cape in little clusters of wings shaped like snowflakes, then stitched eider down into the golden seams. Bubbe dusted it with malachite flakes to bless it from far off Azov, the riches of the earth piling high upon the tsarina's head.

Mama, bubbe, and I were the treasures of Sharon. We were married to our thread, the men and women of Sharon said, and they - from the hunters to the midwives to the rabbi, to my own father, a ship captain and whaler - guarded our secrets with their very lives.

We Weaving Wives were a protected, cherished lot. And our craft was our very soul. But there was a deep magick in that sewing. For in truth, we were good witches. We could summon sunlight to make yellow fabric like a peach. Melt down rusalka hair in our oven to create the finest threads. It was the stuff of legend, our secrets, that we were glad not to tell the rabbi about, or even dear papa. And the menfolk knew better than to ask, but the women always wondered.

The cape was the talk of the kingdom.

No wonder the tsarina was pleased.

As fame of our clothing grew, the Weaving Wives gained esteem, and through charitable works we lifted our community up, filled the synagogue coffers to the brim, and our family did good works in Adonai's name. All so that Peniel – the Face of God – might shine down after the three of us wrestled long with a hill of fabric, like female Jacobs and a needle-bound angel.

But the frost came early that year I turned eighteen, and it stole my bubbe away. As I sat shiva, crying tears like glass beads, I looked into my mirror after shiva was over and found myself a changed maid: my long black curls were winsome, I was plump and rounded to please men, and my cornflower eyes could break hearts. I needed a husband. Only… the village maidens had always been far more winsome.

Fair Shayna, with eyes like silver coins. Comely dark Miriam, with a heart like a thorny rose. And Delilah, the marigold of my garden. I had tossed and turned with all of them in the fields and furrows on Ivan Kupalo, what the Western countries called St. John's Eve, as we searched for fern flowers together to promise bonds of eternal love. Shayna's lips were soft. Miriam's grip on my hot hips was hard, determined, just like Malakh HaMavet striking only holy blows.

But Delilah? She was mother-of-pearl dissolving in Cleopatra's wine. A beauty wrapped in a carpet, delivered to Marc Antony.

I wanted Delilah more than life itself. But Shayna and Miriam had already taken husbands. We were eighteen, after all. Only Delilah, with her red hair, pale skin, full form, and freckles, was left, and to me, she was more holy than any synagogue, a word on the tongue of G-d that would make Chava take an apple all over again, but this time, a blessed fruit. Delilah was a pearl of great price that could redeem. A benediction and wonder that would lighten the load of the Azazel goat on Yom Kippur and set the Temple right.

So, that night in my anger and mourning over losing bubbe too soon, I looked into my mirror, in the flickering light, and I cast a magick spell. I made a wish on bay leaves and some golden rod I had dried earlier that year for Delilah to be mine. As I was threading the bay leaves through a needle, to string them over my dresser, I pricked myself on my thumb.

A bead of red delicious blood bubbled up. Suddenly, the mirror swirled into a gorgeous Ashkenazi royal woman with long black ringlets of hair done up in silver bands, a purple wine-dark dress with gold threading, yellow-green eyes like parched grass, and pale, ghostly skin. Her bruised pink lips were bloody, and there was hunger in her eye.

"Pu pu pu!" I suddenly said, warding off the demon, frightened. I clutched the red thread always tied to my bandeau and threw salt at the mirror. It sizzled as it hit the candle, putting it out. Then, silence.

###

I had not a day before the Queen of Night came to Sharon. She was the talk of our little shtetl, rumored to be disgraced Romanian royalty who had bathed in maiden's blood and newborn calf spittle to retain her youth. She was old, she was young, she was invisible, they whispered. Dressed head to toe in a black veil, riding in a carriage like a hearse. It was pulled by black bulls, and scarlet, bloody-colored ribbons were woven round the four of the black bull's necks.

Just like the blood from my thumb.

Lailah, she was called. I was so lost in fear of her, I did not hear the clinking of bells at our shop, the Weaving Wives. Bubbe was gone, Delilah was not mine, and I was still haunted by a ghost.

I was manning the shop till, daydreaming about the demon. She... had been beautiful. Lailah was said to be hideous. To be virginal and pure. To be a vampir or dhampir or G-d knew what! Only, this Romanian countess or ghost or queen had come to my shop, now, smelling of lavender and patchouli. She had been watching me, and I felt like I was drowning.

A musk radiated off her that reminded me of eating dinner between Delilah's thighs.

Suddenly, Lailah let her veil and robes fall, and the demoness from earlier in the mirror stood naked before me, perfect as a pale statue of Dark Venus, brimstone the farthest word from her.

Her eyes were a poisonous, mesmerizing yellow. Her pubis was lightly thatched with slashes of black, her sex an enticing pink wound. She seemed to be carved from alabaster, her legs ending in owl's feet, great sooty wings on her back, and a night storm cloud of ebon ringlets were set alight to frame her sharp, small and upturned nose and wicked ruby-grapefruit lips.

"Lilith?" I squeaked. I did not have it in me to "Pu pu pu." To reach for metal or iron or salt. To even clutch my red thread.

I knew immediately that if this beautiful, treacherous Queen of the Night asked, I would be her slave. I would be a dog in her yard, licking fruit off her feet, honey off her lips. All to taste... majesty. The divine.

She demurred, smiling to reveal needle teeth that only heightened her beauty. "You have grown beautiful, Jael."

"Oh. No. I, Lilith, with all my pleading, please, flee this place. We are holy. Adonai shall smite you. And you are too beautiful to suffer," I said, rambling, not making sense, soaking in Lilith's beauty, her temptation, her smirk, the way her thick hips and ripe breasts swayed as she walked towards me slowly, like a leopardess stalking its prey.

"But, if I flee, you will be nothing. An adamant bloom plucked too young to thrive. You have all the talent of your bubbe Abigail, and all the strength and industry of your mother Bina. There is a reason our faith is passed on through women, Jael. You are the *perfect* vessel."

I froze. "You mean to possess me?"

Lilith narrowed her yellow eyes at me. Oh, how I wanted to reassure her I was not scared. And yet, I was. Highly terrified. The Witch of Endor was in my shop, and darkness filled the corners, Sheol the depths of the yard, the windows blotted out by the realm of husks. It was only Lilith and I at the axis mundi of the worlds.

"No, I mean to pay you," Lilith laughed in a sultry tone, then she quickly softened. "I have need of a dress for a ball Ashmedai is throwing. Ashmedai and Sammael are both my husbands, but they are at war as of late. I need to dress for battle. For the manner in which I fight, throw the battle, and who I choose as consort, shall determine the course of Kingship in Gehenna."

My jaw dropped. "Like the Maid of Orleans?"

Lilith smiled. "Dear Jael, I have been at this millennia longer than any Frenchwoman. Now, this I must ask you: can you make me a ballgown the color of a mirror, that reflects all it touches, that can withstand hail and hellfire? If you do, you will be wealthier than the tsarina. As you know, the Shekinah often rests with Sammael, and as the Shekinah's Handmaiden, I ascend to G-d in turn. He lets me do what I like, you see. The world, for me, is freedom. As I mean it to be for all women, Jael. Your namesake certainly agreed. We had plans, Jael and I."

"The girl who drove a tent spike through her enemy's head?" I piped out, voice squeaking yet again. I nervously chewed my hair, then spat it out. "Yes, I can make a dress like that. But I do not need riches. Just Delilah."

"Lilah. *Delilah*. She is similar, yet nothing like me. A seal, then, of our bargain?" Lilith leaned against the counter and kissed me, deep. "Yes, you taste just like Jael as well. She was one of mine, you know. Perhaps… but no, Jael. Let sleeping Judges lie."

With that, Lilith disappeared, and the pale, ghostly light of winter trickled into the shop.

I reached for my red thread on my bandeau and snapped it apart, welcoming the demoness in.

For the fabric, I captured moonlight in a jar. I made it slitted at the train, so Lilith could stride across the ballroom of Ashmedai's burning floor like the Queen of Sheba did to win Solomon's heart. For the bodice, I wove it of form-fitting silver silk but loose and dyed from rain under the morning star. Do not ask how the Weaving Wives work our magick. We simply do. It was in bubbe's blood. It is half in mother's blood. And I?

I surpass them both.

I wrote Delilah a letter that night. A letter to come room with me. It did not say much other than "bosom friend" and "bubbe's room is empty" and "mama and papa are leaving for America, so it shall be just us, and I could use a shopkeeper." But I sprayed perfume from

Moscow on it, kissed it thrice, and slipped it in a pink bow and thick sturdy envelope into our hiding tree. An alder.

Delilah wrote me back: "If your gown for this cursed queen goes through, then you will have proven to me that a woman can love a woman, like a man loves a woman, and Jael, I do think… I must not write it."

There were tear stains blotting her delicate signature.

I cried, that night. I stitched Lilith's seam. I used bat wings boiled down to the finest veins for protectant from hellfire. Then I crushed the bay leaves of my witchcraft, when I met Lilith in the mirror, into the fur capelet of mink. It was my heart's treasure. My greatest wish of all.

And finally, a hilt for a dagger, bejeweled with malachite from Mount Azov. It was sacred in Russia, from one Mistress – the Mistress of Copper Mountain – to the Queen of Night.

Lilith came the day after Sabbath.

She tried it on, the silk bunching around her in pleasing, curvaceous angles, the embroidery and pearls and malachite and mink sparkling, and she shone like the tsarina's silver tiara.

Lilith smiled in the mirror: "It's perfect, my Jael. Come walk with me."

Into her dark midnight carriage with the four red-banded black bulls I went. We rode to Gehenna. What I saw would frighten Enoch himself. Dumah, at the gate, with his poisoned sword of gall. Hazarmavet, the Court of the Dead, where new souls ate meat and drank wine in perfect silence. The winnowing of souls in the fire of Sheol with the punishing, purifying angels. A glimpse of Gan Eden and the Silver City where the angels lived, attending the Promised Messiah. It was all like a crack in the sky.

Finally, Ashmedai's realm. A realm of exotic desert fruit and pleasure girls and winebearer ephebes. Hot searing heat, simoom winds, oases and belly dancers. It was scandalous.

Sammael's forces of death, poison and decay camped at the door. I waited in the carriage as Lilith walked on French heels to the forefront, her dagger held high, her dress that I had painstakingly, feverishly sewed gleaming under the hot desert sun.

Lilith's beauty sparked Sammael's shedim and lilim and seirim into frenzy. They descended on Ashmedai's forces as the demon king emerged from his glistening sandstone palace with his forces, dates and palm and rivers of jewels surrounding us on all four sides.

I watched as Lilith turned the tides of the battle, flirted with Ashmedai, lured Sammael. In the end, Lilith took both Ashmedai and Sammael's crowns as they kneeled and kissed her hands off their heads. She melted the coronets down with fiery breath from her beautiful lips, then formed two gold arm bands for her pale limbs.

It seemed Gehenna had a new ruler.

I am old now. Delilah is my bosom companion. I talk to Lilith in the mirror, late at night, I am aged, Lilith is ageless, and she tells me tales of the world: the invention of electricity. War in America. Discoveries in Asia. How her plans are in motion to free women, so one day, we are not so tied to the cycles of our womb, forced to labor in birth pangs like Chavah.

Delilah and I adopt three girls and teach them the secrets of weaving, sewing, and stitchery. We are bringing the crafts of our shtetl into a new age. My parents died in America and seemed to have prospered. I have no intention of leaving Karelia. We are the exclusive gownmakers for the new tsarina.

It is a good life. It is a small life. Lilith and Adonai shower riches upon our community – not too much, but enough that Sharon is known as blessed. The Shekinah still roosts with Sammael, and will until the Temple is set right, and Her people ascend.

I am happy all my days. So is Delilah. When we die, we are led by Lilith the Perpetual Regent of Gehenna to be her personal weavers and outfitters, and our daughter's daughter's daughters know true freedom in the modern age.

And all because Lilith sewed the seam.

Allister Nelson

Allister Nelson (she/her) is a poet and author whose work has appeared in Apex Magazine, The Showbear Family Circus, Eternal Haunted Summer, Bibliotheca Alexandrina, SENTIDOS: Revistas Amazonicas, Black Sheep: Unique Tales of Terror and Wonder, The Kaidankai Ghost Podcast, Wicked Shadow Press's Halloweenthology, The Greyhound Journal, FunDead Publications' Gothic Anthology, POWER Magazine, Renewable Energy World, and many other venues.

So Long As We Still Live

Paul Leone

When the call came, Józefa Wojcik was expecting it. She'd rehearsed it in her mind a half-dozen times, which ended up helping not one damn bit.

"Oh," she said. "Okay. I'll be there as soon –" she choked up for a second "soonasIcan."

She hung up and hurried out into the bleak morning. The sky was a sheet of angry grey clouds, typical for this time of year.

"You're listening to WVAR and now here's the Top of the Morning News," the woman on the radio declared in a far too eager voice. "In Washington, Congressional hearings continue for Supreme Court nominee –"

Józefa grunted, switched the radio off and drove down the dark streets in silence. After a few minutes, she pulled onto the highway. The only people other than her out at this hour were the snowplows. Józefa fell in behind one and then gritted her teeth and passed it, despite the slush and ice on the highway.

On and on went Federal 44, out of Orchard Park, past the new Buffalo Airport, past the sprawling Curtiss-Wright factory complex straddling the OP/West Seneca line, past the stadium, and finally into Lackawanna. She left the highway, passed a cemetery, a seminary, and a preschool, probably some kind of metaphor there, and then hung a right onto a side street. There was the hospital. OLV – Our Lady of Victory.

Every time she came there, every time she read the name, Józefa wondered if it hurt the local Poles – the ones born there, the ones who remembered. There was no victory for them, no miracle of Lepanto, no miracle of the Vistula, only defeat, exile and, one by one, death in foreign lands.

Józefa parked across the street and then jogged over to the big red-brick building.

The woman working the front desk recognized both Józefa and the look on her face. "Go on up, hon," she said. "I'll sign you in."

Józefa murmured her thanks as she hurried to the elevator. She stabbed the button for the sixth floor and shifted from one foot to the other as the elevator slowly climbed up.

A soft chime pinged and each number flashed a little as the floors went by.

Józefa shut her eyes for a second. She remembered the time he'd seen her off to Camp Barlow for Basic Training, wondered how he felt, wondered if he somehow hoped things would go wrong and she'd end up shooting Germans. Probably not. But...

Jesus, what's wrong with me?

Józefa exhaled, opened her eyes, as the elevator came to a halt and the doors slid open.

605 was two left turns and then eight doors down a long hallway from the elevator.

She pushed her way into the room and took it all in.

A nurse she sort of knew, a doctor she definitely knew and liked and hated at the same time, and the hospital chaplain, a young Nigerian-American priest.

And on the bed, silent and asleep, her grandfather Zdzisław Wisniewski, her dear old *dziadzia*. He was dying, had been dying for two years, and now this was it.

"Good morning, detective," Dr. Makowski murmured.

Józefa nodded at him, at the nurse and at the priest, all at once, then looked at the little man on the hospital bed. *How did you get so* small, *dziadzia?* she asked herself. In her memories, in her mind's eye, he was still the big ex-boxer, the former Marine who carried her around on his shoulders.

She balled her fists, clenched them tight, nails digging into her palms. It turned out she'd only *thought* she'd gotten used to, accepted, the thing that was eating him up from the inside, making the big man a little thing beneath a thin, starchy sheet, a little person surrounded by machines and tubes.

"Morning," Józefa mumbled.

"It will not be very long now," Father Usanga said in a low voice.

Józefa nodded. She crossed her arms over her chest and hugged herself. "Is he... has he woken up at all since last night?"

That had been rough. Just her and him, and Father Usanga administering the Last Rites.

She wondered if *dziadzia* even knew what was going on. He'd spoken, but softly, in broken peasant Polish that Józefa couldn't quite understand. Did he know? Did it hurt?

"I'm sorry, he hasn't," Dr. Makowski said.

Józefa heaved a sigh and rubbed her eyes for a minute. "Yeah. Okay." She sighed again. "I want to sit with him. Alone."

"Of course. We'll be right out in the hallway."

Józefa nodded and turned her back to the door as the three left as quietly as they could.

She lifted up the plastic and faux-leather chair and pulled it closer to the bed, then sat down.

"Hello, *dziadzia.* It's me, it's – hnh – it's Little Josie," she said as she leaned closer to him. There was no movement except the painfully shallow rise and fall of his chest as he breathed with the help of the machines. His eyes were closed, his lips open only enough to let in a tube. "I'm here. It's morning now, you know? Looks like it's gonna snow again."

The EKG next to the bed beeped softly every couple seconds.

Józefa gently laid her hand atop his small, liver-spotted one.

"Your turkeys were out again last night. I saw them down by the creek." She took a deep breath, held it, exhaled. "And the deer, too. Tracks all over the side of the driveway." *Dziadzia* and his deer. Up until six or seven years ago, when his knees got bad, he went hunting up in the Adirondacks. But the deer that lived in the woods around his house, those were practically his pets. It didn't make any damn sense to her.

The EKG kept beeping, softly, steadily. Józefa lifted her eyes from his face and stared at the monitor.

It was getting slower. The beeps just a little farther apart.

She shivered and shut her eyes for a second, then opened them and looked down.

"I remember the song you taught me when I was little. What you sang when I cried." She took a ragged breath and leaned forward a little more. "*Jeszcze Polska nie zginęła, Kiedy my żyjemy, Co nam obca przemoc wzięła, Szablą odbierzemy.*"

Memories rose up into her mind's eye. The two of them fishing in the little green pond by his house, or else on Neuman Creek just up the road. They'd gone fishing the day after her parents were buried at Holy Sepulchre. That was when he'd taught her the song, the anthem, really, but to her it was just The Song.

"*Marsz, marsz, Dąbrowski, Z ziemi włoskiej do Polski, Za twoim przewodem, Złączym się z narodem.*"

A white dress, a lacy veil, new shoes, flowers, the altar rail of Our Lady of Exile, the Eucharist for the first time, looking back and seeing him there in his old uniform, all the colorful badges and bars, the five gold stripes on his shoulders, standing at attention with the biggest smile in the world on his face.

"*Przejdziem Wisłę, przejdziem Wartę, Będziem Polakami, Dał nam przykład Bonaparte, Jak zwyciężać mamy.*"

Graduations. Ellicott Road Middle School, Orchard Park Central High, Basic Training, the Buffalo Police Academy. No matter what, he was there, either in the uniform he loved to wear (*especially* at an Army ceremony) or the suit he hated to wear.

"*Marsz, marsz, Dąbrowski, Z ziemi włoskiej do Polski. Za twoim przewodem, Złączym się z narodem.*"

Baking pierogi together, either in the little old house on Dartmouth Avenue in the city or else the house by the pond later on. The time she remembered best had been just after Zofia's funeral. They'd been married forty years, since even before he came to America, and Józefa came into the kitchen and saw him just standing there, looking so lost. And crying. The only time she'd ever seen him cry.

"Jak Czarniecki do Poznania... Po szwedzkim zaborze... Dla ojczyzny ratowania... Wrócim się przez morze."

Going to Bombers games at the old Gioia Stadium downtown. When she was a kid, all the way through high school, it was the same every Sunday. Mass, then either heading into the city to watch the home games or back home for the away games. Three months ago had been the last time. The Bombers played the Bears and squeezed out a win in overtime. He'd fallen asleep in the third quarter and woke up afterwards, mistaking her for someone who'd been dead for twenty years. She'd cried most of the way home from the nursing home.

The beeping of the EKG was slower still now.

"Marsz, marsz, Dąbrowski, Z ziemi włoskiej do Polski. Za twoim przewodem, Złączym się z narodem."

All the stories he told. Stories about his days in the Marines — boot camp, being stationed in the south of England, two tours in Burma. Stories about his boxing days — the time he met Sonny Liston, the time he knocked out Malik Wilder in the eighth round, the time he went twelve rounds with Golden Joe Kavanaugh.

"Już tam ojciec do swej Basi, Mówi zapłakany — Słuchaj jeno, pono nasi, Biją w tarabany."

All the stories he didn't tell. The family, the old country, the war, the camp, sneaking across 2000 miles of Nazi-occupied Europe, the sister he'd lost along the way (a great-aunt that Józefa didn't even know she had until six years ago). Stories he didn't tell, stories she'd never asked about, and now never could. Little pieces of Poland lost forever.

"Marsz, marsz, Dąbrowski, Z ziemi włoskiej do Polski. Za twoim przewodem, Złączym się z narodem..."

The soft beeping stopped. The room was silent now.

* * *

WISNIEWSKI – Gunnery Sergeant Zdzisław, USMC (ret)

Of Orchard Park, NY on January 15, 2018. 91 years old. Born in Labiszyn, Poland. Devoted husband of the late Zofia Wisniewski. Loving father of the late Antek Wisniewski and late Marta Wojcik (nee Wisniewski). Adored grandfather of Józefa Wojcik. Friends will be received 4-8 PM, Friday, at AMARANTE FUNERAL HOME, 6404 West Quaker Street, Orchard Park, NY, 716-555-9320. A Requiem Mass will be held on Saturday, 9:30 AM at Our Lady of Exile Church, Orchard Park. Please assemble at church. In lieu of flowers, donations may be made to the Polish Roman Catholic Union of America.

"Mazurek Dąbrowskiego" ("Dąbrowski's Mazurka")

Jeszcze Polska nie zginęła,	Poland has not yet perished,
Kiedy my żyjemy.	So long as we still live.
Co nam obca przemoc wzięła,	What the foreign force has taken from us,
Szablą odbierzemy.	We shall with sabre retrieve.
Marsz, marsz, Dąbrowski,	March, march, Dąbrowski,
Z ziemi włoskiej do Polski.	From the Italian land to Poland.
Za twoim przewodem	Under your command
Złączym się z narodem.	We shall rejoin the nation.

Przejdziem Wisłę, przejdziem Wartę,	We'll cross the Vistula, we'll cross the Warta,
Będziem Polakami.	We shall be Polish.
Dał nam przykład Bonaparte,	Bonaparte has given us the example
Jak zwyciężać mamy.	Of how we should prevail.
Marsz, marsz, Dąbrowski,	March, march, Dąbrowski,
Z ziemi włoskiej do Polski.	From the Italian land to Poland.
Za twoim przewodem	Under your command
Złączym się z narodem.	We shall rejoin the nation.
Jak Czarniecki do Poznania	Like Czarniecki to Poznań
Po szwedzkim zaborze,	After the Swedish annexation,
Dla ojczyzny ratowania	To save our homeland,
Wrócim się przez morze.	We shall return across the sea.
Marsz, marsz, Dąbrowski,	March, march, Dąbrowski,
Z ziemi włoskiej do Polski.	From the Italian land to Poland.
Za twoim przewodem	Under your command
Złączym się z narodem.	We shall rejoin the nation.

Już tam ojciec do swej Basi	A father, in tears,
Mówi zapłakany –	Says to his Basia
Słuchaj jeno, pono nasi	Listen, our boys are said
Biją w tarabany.	To be beating the tarabans.
Marsz, marsz, Dąbrowski,	March, march, Dąbrowski,
Z ziemi włoskiej do Polski.	From the Italian land to Poland.
Za twoim przewodem	Under your command
Złączym się z narodem.	We shall rejoin the nation.

Paul Leone

Paul Leone grew up on a strange diet of Tolkien, Lewis, Lucas, Roddenberry, Stoker, monster movies and comic books. This genre passion has inexplicably fused with his entrance into the Catholic Church to give you the world of the Immortal Champions and his other weird tales. He currently resides in Western New York with a cat who is not at all interested in his overly large collection of bad movies.

His author website is
paul-leone.com

Pet Words - Poems About Our Pets

Various Authors

Dom Morgan

Rest with Jodi, our beautiful old girl, Lil. More than 20 years on this earth you never had a bad day and brought so much joy. I took this photo the day before she left us and wrote the poem below yesterday, the day she went home.

It's only a cat.
But she's my cat. She. Well she was, because she died today. We cried today. We cried for her, over her. Our tears pooling on her fur. Her matted fur, hanging baggy around her ancient bones. Old. Fragile and so very bare. She wasn't ours. Because nobody owns a cat, you see. Free spirited between you and me and if you love and truly understand the feline kind you'll agree. With me... that nobody owns a cat.
We lay with her, one day, many years ago... as a younger cat.... on the dusty wooden floor, holding a paw.. each.. my wife and I as she birthed her fur babies. Our fur babies.. on our dusty wooden floor. And when her best friend, Jodi, our beautiful little girl was ill and died, we all again cried. But not the cat.. because they don't do that. They don't shed tears or weep... or show their feelings like us humans show. Yet they mourn.. and mourn she did, on our daughters empty bed. Her fur shed. As she gnawed and tugged at her coat, for days and days, never.leaving Jodis bed, like I said. Mourning. Weeping metophorically, categorically gnawing and tugging at her fur till almost bare, a semi hairless cat grieving. But she was never ours. And today we let her go.

Jay Wolfe

Ode To Reese

Patriarch, kind and gentle
Loving of his clan
Aged warrior, old survivor
Beloved of his people

Farewell Reese, you served your feline folk
You warmed your human friends
You lived beyond the end of times
An ode to Reese I sing

Goodbye my one-time friend
Unseen these many years
Your tales of fun and winsome jinks
I heard but on the phone

Sadly passed from the earthly realm
You surely abide in a feline heaven
Reunited with your bairns and clanfolk
Farewell Reese, you served your people well

28-10-13

Photo of Reese and his daughter Sophie

Old Fluffy Dusty Cat

old fluffy dusty cat
you sit on top my cupboard
never complaining
rubbing your white little paws together
fluffy tail dangling
a sign, a symbol
of my continuing life
for I saved you from the bin
old fluffy dusty cat
old fluffy dusty cat

once you were a beloved toy
but now you have no resale value
donation to a charity shop
you were surely up for the chop
I couldn't let it be
I took you home with me
old fluffy dusty cat
old fluffy dusty cat

while I live free you have a home
no child ever to play with you
but no rotting rubbish heap
no cruncher in the dustcart's rear
just a home, a place upon a cupboard top
a base for you, my little grey friend
old fluffy dusty cat
old fluffy dusty cat

Simon R. Gladdish

Illustrated by Rusty Gladdish

Cat Limericks

We have a small kitten called Minky

Who's incredibly smart, cute and dinky;

He's extremely affectionate

And thinks being stroked is great

But when he gets in his tray, he's quite stinky!

I noticed that she

Had got stuck in a tree;

Though I could barely see her

I did my best to free her

Then rewarded us both with a nice cup of tea.

I enter the lounge with a sinking heart;

The kittens are tearing the place apart.

Their mum (asleep on a chair)

Clearly couldn't care

As she alternates purrs, snores and farts.

If I stay as still as can be,

The kitten will sit on my knee

But when I move

Or try to improve

My position, he jumps off the settee.

Dragonfly Days in Provence – by Rusty Gladdish

The cat had a crap

And then sat on my lap;

I was feeling rather glum

As she hadn't wiped her bum

And I'm a fastidious chap.

You stupid thing!

Stop bothering

Me. I've fed you twice,

There's loads of mice -

So go and do some scavenging.

Red Riding Hood (edited) – Rusty Gladdish

I sometimes think that I could be a cat

(A handsome lap-cat who was rather fat.)

They know how to kill,

They never pay a bill

And it doesn't take them long to smell a rat.

Our cat puts her paws

Together to give herself a round of applause;

She is a very intelligent cat

(There is no doubt about that!)

Why some days she can even open doors.

We know that it's dry in the kennel

And equally dry in the tunnel

But Buster's insane!

He camps out in the rain

And might just as well swim in the Channel.

Our Minnie has had a hard life

(Her children and grandchildren are rife!)

Yet she never complains,

Stays at home and remains

A delight to myself and my wife.

Our hearts were filled with sorrow

When we gave up Minky and Minnow;

Though ideally we still need them,

We could not afford to feed them

And now we feel it's time for them to grow.

Just Another Poppy Day – Rusty Gladdish

We had to use some flattery

To get our kitten in the cattery;

He wasn't very happy

To leave his Mam and Pappy

And claimed assault and battery.

I watched our cats today and it was weird -

The 'orange monster' had appeared;

This cat was bad

So they fought like mad

Until the electric air was thoroughly cleared.

Our kitten Minky has teeth sharp as needles;

Around our living room he often speedles.

He's as sweet as can be

And will sleep on your knee

But only if you remember his feedles.

An acquaintance of mine named Nat

Opined - Curiosity killed the cat;

I answered - I know that,

You nonsensical gnat!

Whereupon he concluded our chat.

Buster,

You don't pass muster!

Let me tell you to your face

That you're an embarrassing disgrace

And I'm bored with your endless bluster.

(From: Ludicrous Limericks, Ridiculous Limericks and Nonsensical Limericks - 2023)

Paintings by Rusty Gladdish

Grey Wolf

Huntress

White furred feline prowling ,
Hunting for her prey ,
In the humid green of undergrowth
The royal terraces abut .
Emerald , her eyes shine in the darkness -
Saole , royal pet of kings .
The warm softness of her nudging head ,
Ripples of muscle in her side ,
Every eye takes in her majesty ;
A cat for power symbolised -
Killer or a loving friend .

10-3-1993

TOUCHED ALWAYS
(NEVER DESERTING YOU)

And here you are, and there you are
Always in my memory, ever on my mind
Adorning walls, my photographs
To keep my soul alive.
Never a day without a thought
Nor one without the wish
Though this be house, you're at my home,
I often wish I were
To hold you tight, to cuddle you
To stroke the fur, to hear you purr
Miaow...

February 1994

MIAOW

The eyes so bright tonight
Miaow
She prowls her domain,
A cock of the head
A twitch of the ear,
Intruder alert!
Miaow!

August 1993

2 Juniper – The Later Interior

One-Place Study

Whilst the shape of the house affected the development of the rooms, the addition of the utility room itself in 1978 was an extension of the early interior. I can only just remember when the kitchen door opened up onto the side path, bounded by the wall, riding my tractor up and down it, but by the time I was in 2nd Year Juniors the extension was built, and was home to our cats, Tandy and Tiddles.

The second expansion of the house, that of turning the study into my sister's bedroom, extended out over the utility room, and adding a porch to the front of the house, occurred at the start of the 1980s, and can be looked at as entering the later phase. It can be noted that the décor of the porch certainly changed over the years, and we can map this development through photographs. But that of my sister's bedroom remained pretty much unchanged until she left home – more fans on the wall, over time, the addition of some pop star posters, such as Donny Osmond in his leathers, but the same furniture, carpet and layout from when the room was first created.

Conversely, the building of the lounge extension occurred in 1984, some eight years after the construction of the house and a decade or so before my parents sold it, so can generally be considered as part of the later development of the interior. Plenty of photographs from earlier years show the lounge wall as the outside wall, with the unit, the bar football game, and the television up against it. The opening up of the extra space, fully a 50% addition to the lounge, allowed the unit to move into the extension, along with the record player we had inherited from my Grandpa, and the TV cupboard that was superceded by a new television, but with its open-out doors proved to be a useful piece of furniture in its own right, once devoid of its electronic interior.

Alex the Rabbit, won on the evening of the 4th October 1986 at the East Community Centre, became a permanent feature of the lounge extension, seated usually upon one of the chairs that came from my paternal grandparents – presumably when my Grandma moved to Croydon, she downsized and donated this, and other furniture, to us. The other major element of the lounge extension was the brown folding-out chair that could be made into a spare bed, and which was remarkably comfortable. This was always positioned to face into the rest of the lounge, so anyone who sat in it was included in any conversation going on, and could, depending on where the migrating television was located, sometimes watch it.

Then there was the attic, or loft as we usually called it, more accessible in later years with a drop-down ladder, and floored over with floorboards, laid by Dad. Whilst a storage space, it was also accessible if you wanted to go through what you had stored up there, or to find things that Mum and Dad had squirreled away in the past but had an interest in now.

Beyond the extensions, and opening up of the loft, the main developments to look at across the interior of the house are changes to:-
- carpets
- furniture
- wallpaper
- doors
- layout

Doors might be the most intriguing place to start. Very early on, so early I don't remember what it was like beforehand, Dad changed the kitchen door into the hall into a sliding door, that slid into a recess inside the kitchen. This obviously freed up a lot of space, and a sliding door was the design added between the kitchen and utility room when the latter was built.

Not long after, the bathroom door was also put onto a runner hung outside the bathroom, something which visitors did not always remember and numerous times they would push the door when finished with their ablutions, only for it to come off the track and hang waiting for one of us to pop it back up.

Somewhat later the door between the kitchen and the dining room was also transformed into a sliding door, which certainly opened up the corner of the dining room behind it, which had previously been somewhat blocked off every time the door was open.

Eventually, the double doors between the lounge and the dining room were also converted into sliding doors, though retaining their ornamental handles. With the runner set into the lounge, above the doors, this had the effect of closing a slice of the lounge carpet into the dining room space every time they were closed.

We will take it in turn to look at the rooms, as photographs allow, tracking their development from the mid 1980s to the mid 1990s. Some things always seemed to remain the same – the bureau in the dining room, with the clock atop of it, never moved in 18 years. It had the perfect position, filled the space to the right of the window perfectly, and there was never any need, or use, in changing it. Conversely, sideboards, cupboards, and the piano in the same room regularly seemed to take a trip around the different walls, though the central dining table, which we had bought for the house in Stalbridge, always remained the same.

The carpet of the main lounge area never changed, but those of most of the rest of the house did over time. There are no direct photographs of the shower room/downstairs toilet, but to the best of my knowledge nothing ever changed in there – the green square carpet tiles, the ceramic area in front of the shower, the tiles upon one wall, the sink and unit, the toilet where behind it in the mould I could see the face of Jesus, though he did not come out well when I tried to photograph him.

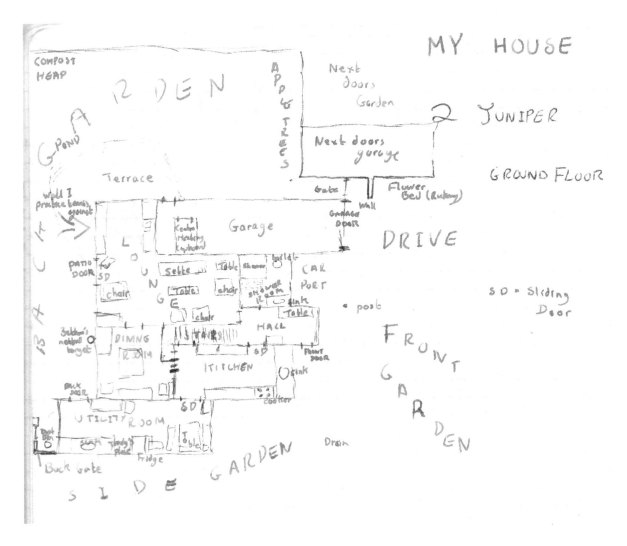

This floorplan of the downstairs and some of the garden area was drawn up by me in the early Summer of 1986, and placed at the back of my diary. It is pretty close to a scale drawing, and the locations of furniture etc upon it provide a snapshot of that time.

There is a single photograph of the understairs cupboard, taken because our cat Tandy was hiding at the back, behind all the bags and things stored in the far area where the ceiling came almost down to the floor.

Likewise, only one photograph allows us to see into the shower room, slightly, so the plan above offers our only real look at the placing of the elements within that room. A rectangular high window opened out into the car port, offering light dependant on whether a vehicle was parked in its way. Our white Buccanneer motorhome could park itself under the carport, the later larger motorhomes tended to abutt into it from the driveway.

The Kitchen

Here we see the little "breakfast bar" that was used as a telephone table for the telephone upon the wall. The sliding door is to the right, and the stools stored underneath it.

The radiator at the end of the kitchen, also showing the door to the utility room on the left, and to the dining room on the right.

My sister cooking in the kitchen. Nothing much in this picture changed over the years – the venetial blind, here shown shut, was the same as always. The cooker was a new one from when we first moved in, but this one pictured remained in use for well over a decade, and was the one I cooked food on from my mid teens. The work surfaces, the cupboard fronts, the sink, the orange tiles Dad put in, and the carpet floor tiles all remained the same.

What did change over the years were the kettle and the toaster, the location of spice cupboard or kitchen utensil rack, the kitchen scales, whether the Soda-Stream came out for a long while, or if it lived mostly in the cupboard. The telephone shown previously changed over time from a dialler, to one with buttons, then later to one with an answer-phone on a small cassette.

A wider view of the kitchen, showing Mum by the scales upon the wall, and the spice rack over on the right, with a fire extinguisher above, that we thankfully never had to use. We can see here the whole array of the kitchen cupboards, including the tall floor-to-ceiling one on the left, and the other overhead ones on the right. A similar view below with our Aunty Syvlia in, allowing us a clearer look at the cooker.

Above, my Mum and sister cooking in the kitchen, showing the whole length of the window behind them, and the cooker's grill (at the top) opened up. Below, my sister at the sink showing details of that, the venetian blind here open, and the storage area on top of the cooker. We also get a different angle on this corner of the kitchen, under the cupboard.

Here, my sister is baking, and we can see the wall with the scales and the double-plug, and to the right, the kitchen roll holder on the wall, and the brown kitchen bin under the counter. It also gives a good impression of how the door to the utility room and the radiator fit in.

Here is a view to the rarely-photographed left of the kitchen sink, also showing the window sill in orange tiles, and a view out at the tree in the front garden.

The Utility Room

Mum down the far end of the utility room in the early 1980s, showing (rather unusually!) the ceiling and the light fitting, and what was on top of the cupboard above the washing machine. In the later photo below, the wall has been painted from blue to yellow, and we have a second freezer which goes where Tandy's food area used to be. The tumble dryer, much to Tandy's pleasure, remained in good use and condition for the whole time that we lived there.

Above, we can see the backdoor into the utility room, and the step up to it that my cousins are standing upon. Below, Tandy's feeding area moved on top of the worktop with the arrival of the second freezer, here clearly seen beneath the wall cupboard.

The Hall and the Porch

Whilst we generally termed the extension the porch extension in the early 1980s, we continued to refer to the room within it as the hall, simply as an enlarged version of what it had been before.

This early photograph would be from when the hall extension was new, and is shown to compare with later photographs below. The pillar on the right is where the original external wall of the house was, and to its right, just out of shot is the floor-to-ceiling shoe cupboard, that back at the earliest iteration of the house was the location of the telephone before my Dad rooted that into the kitchen.

This photograph is pretty much a direct comparison with the one above, and shows a new carpet, which was laid not only in the hall but up the stairs and on the landing as well, and new wallpaper. The hall cupboard is also clearly visible here, as is the barometer upon the wall, and the rubber plant in the corner. The wooden table remains the same. Below, Tandy poses.

In the above photograph we can see the hall radiator, shelf (with Tandy) and mirror, and on the left the door into the shower room. In the photo below of Dad, we can see that the new wallpaper continues up the stairs

The Shower Room

No photographs into the shower room seem to exist, so these elements snipped from other photographs can give us the merest hint.

These tiles are on the wall to the left of the door as you enter, with the shower immediately in front of you.

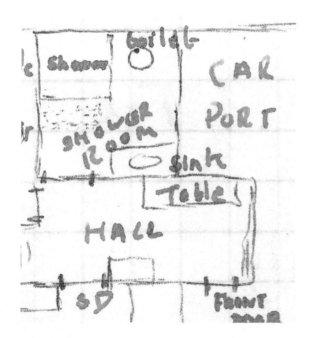

The layout of the shower room can be seen in this section of the ground floor plan of the house. The speckled area in front of the shower are ceramic tiles upon the floor, to step out onto. The rest of the flooring was square green carpet tiles.

The Stairs

Above, looking up the stairs from the bottom at Tandy sleeping snugly on them. Below, looking down the stairs from the landing at my sister coming up the stairs. You can see behind her the stairs shelf, where at one point I had some of my model aeroplanes, but which in this photograph is populated with collectible pencil sharpeners in the shape of old fashioned objects.

Dining Room

The dining room lay at the corner at the back of the house between the kitchen and the lounge. It looked out onto the back garden, the roses, daffodils, and the plum tree in the corner.

The piano tended to move around between the wall to the right of the kitchen door, and to here pictured above, on the left of the kitchen door. It would eventually settle for good in the position below, due to the purchase of a new unit for the dining room.

Compare the picture above from Christmas 1984 with that below from several years later. Where we see Mum and Aunty Sylvia, we can now see the new unit behind them, permanently against that wall, and on the left the enclosure for the sliding door. With that corner of the room now opened up, plates and other display items could be placed there and seen without danger of being hidden by the opening door.

The photograph above shows Dad with the Subbuteo set, Christmas 1992, showing the rocking chair still in its corner by the window. The photograph below shows the final sliding doors created by Dad, those between the dining room and lounge, as Mum and Aunty Sylvia play Keyword.

The above photograph fills in the missing corner, showing little change since 1976, with the bureau safely in position there, and the clock within it. The other side of the new sliding doors can also be seen. Below, Alex makes a rare foray into the dining room for a celebration.

The Lounge

These photographs show aspects of the wandering television. In the above, it is in the corner nearest to the dining room (here shown with the sliding doors in place). Below, it is in the corner on the wall which the lounge shares with the shower room.

The top photograph from Dad's 50th Birthday Party in September 1983 shows the double doors from the lounge into the dining room. The bottom photograph, a few years later, shows the doors still as normal doors, but here both are closed as Mum and Dad pose in front of them before a night out.

This photograph of Tandy beneath the radiator shows well the pattern on the lounge carpet which never changed throughout the 18 years of occupancy.

This photograph shows the television in its more usual position, adjoining the lounge extension, with the two shelves either side of the extension having upon them the speakers for the record player. Sometimes they both worked at the same time! But this was never certain. The cupboard on the right of this picture was made by Dad from the wood of the original wardrobe in his and Mum's bedroom, when they replaced it with a new one.

The above photograph looks towards the door into the hall, and shows Grandma visiting, and cuddling with Tandy. In this later period, the sofa at the back, part of a set with the chair seen in the foreground, generally sat mostly on that far wall, though occasionally it moved to be against the left-hand wall.

This view of my cousins visiting acts as a transition between photographs of the lounge proper, where they are seated (albeit photographed from the dining room), and the following photographs of the Lounge Extension.

Lounge Extension

The above photograph is a good view of one side of the Lounge Extension, showing Alex on his Spanish chair, the brown fold-out sleeping chair, and Dad by the drinks cupboard. The photo below of Mum and Dad shows the other side, with the record player and bookcase.

Tandy on the turtle, showing how the record storage kind of over-flowed as me and my sister got into buying them, here being arranged under Alex's chair.

My sister and Tandy in the lounge extension in later years.

The Landing

It would seem, logically enough, that nobody really took photographs of the landing unless they were taking photographs of Tandy upon the landing.

The main things to note are that the carpet and wallpapers changed when those of the hall, and staircase did too, and the presence of the airing cupboard, the orange door on the right at the bottom, which was in the centre of the landing, directly facing you as you came up the stairs.

The Bathroom

The only known full photograph of the bathroom was taken in 1994 when my parents were selling the house. It does a good job of showing everything. The tiles above the bath taps, disrupting the blue and brown patterning, were mirrored, allowing the bather to see themselves, steam willing. The partial photo at the bottoms shows the tilings opposite the sink, and the clothes line that could stretch across the bath up high.

The Study

Not that many pictures seem to have been taken of the study either, but we can do our best with the ones below.

This is a good view that shows how the study was the centre of Dad's writing and accounting life, with the filing cabinet, the shelves full of folders, the typewriter on the desk, and the layout perfect for his use. The dark blue curtains remained the same throughout the life of the room. Below, my sister works on the Brother electric typewriter, now nearer to the door, showing also the books on the nearer shelves.

My Sister's Bedroom

As mentioned before, there were no notable changes in the décor of my sister's room after she moved from what became the study into the newly extended bedroom, reaching out across the utility room extension, at the start of the 1980s. Even the specific location of furniture remained the same. She may have photographs from inside the room from when she was young, but those I have tend to be from when she was mid to late teens, and many are from when she had left home and was either back for a while, or was back to go through her things.

The above photograph is a starting point from around when my sister moved into the room, showing her love of fans, which would spread out upon the wall above her bed, here linked to her dancing in the outfit she is wearing.

We can see a heated towel rail to one side, and that the bed has built-in shelves on either side (it was symmetrical).

This photograph shows my sister with Humphrey the bear, which she won in a church 'guess the name of the bear' competition. It was Humbert, but nobody guessed that, and her guess of Humphrey was the closest, so she brought this much-beloved white bear home. Unfortunately the camera I took this photograph with did not do indoor photographs well, but I include this one as it the only other one contemporaneous to when my sister was living at home, and also the only one showing what was down the left-hand side of the bed, before the window that looked out upon the area of utility room roof that the bathroom window also did (top left below)

This photograph is from after my sister had moved out and was back sorting things, which is why older family photographs are upon the walls, but it shows the position of the bed, the heated towel rail, and the sink with cupboards etc well. Below, Tandy upon her bed, with the sink unit behind.

The below picture again dates from after my sister had moved out, but shows the bookshelves at the end of the room, and the bureau unit on the right that were always there whilst my sister was at home.

The same again with this picture above, which shows the bureau and my sister, but after she moved out. She would not have had the pictures up on the wall above it while she was there!

Mum and Dad's Bedroom

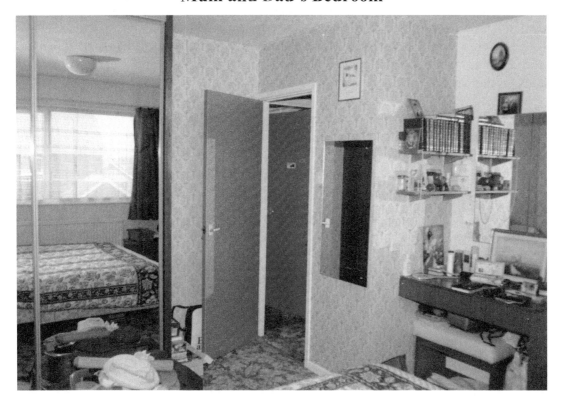

The above photograph must have been taken from the far side of my parents' bed, looking back towards the door onto the landing. We can see on the left the wardrobe with the mirrored doors, which replaced the older all-wood one, and in those mirrored doors we can see the bed. We can see the mirror on the wall, beside the door, and the dressing table which for many of the years we were there also had the black and white television perched upon it.

Above, a photograph of the bedhead, showing the wallpaper all round the room, and the green tin which always held Rich Tea biscuits.

My Bedroom

Before 1981, at least, my bedroom had a completely different look to it. I remember at my 11th birthday party, everyone able to crowd in, the red worktop down the side with the ZX81 set up on. But even then, I think my bed must have moved into the middle of the room as I remember anger at Star Trek minerals I had drawn and shoved under the bed, and pictures from Uggie of spaceships on the back of the door.

There are no known photographs of my bedroom in its early years. Camera film was more expensive then and the cameras that I and my sister had as children generally only took photographs outside. Only from the mid 1980s onwards did we have cameras that might work inside, and money to devote to developing film as a hobby, rather than a holiday memory.

These photographs, therefore, generally reflect the late 1980s to 1994, during which I went to university at term-time and came home in the holidays (mostly), and then lived 1992-1993 at home before going away again for good.

The room had always had a high degree of decoration, with postcards and posters added as I got them, but from 1988 onwards it also received those of my university living, squeezing into every available space with blu-tak until taken off again to return to my room away from home.

Above, looking over the bed at the small colour television which dominated that corner, and which replaced my grandparents' ancient black and white television that had had UHF and VHF dials upon it. This colour TV could be attached to the ZX Spectrum computer (adjacent in the dropdown unit) or be used to watch programmes that were different from those being watched in the lounge downstairs on the main TV.

A rare photograph of the far corner of the room, showing the curtains in good detail, and the array of posters on the wardrobe door. The cupboard on the left of the photograph was a later addition, housing mainly history books as my collection grew – previously this whole area between the bed and the window had been available for wargaming, and setting up dioramas upon the floor.

The wardrobe had built-in drawers in the middle, and a shelf up high. As kids we were able to climb up to the top and sort of sit up there. I remember one time with a friend doing so, and my parents had stored Duty Free packs of cigarettes, those foot-long cellophane-wrapped multi-packs, bought for my grandparents.

Tandy on the window ledge, from which she (and me!) could access the garage roof.

My sister playing cards on the bed, with behind her my badge board, with the collection bought on holidays around the country and pinned up.

My Grandma bought me the keyboard as a 21st birthday present, so this photograph of my sister playing it dates to 1992. You can see it here resting upon the top of the by then not new cupboard. Below, a photograph of me in my "desk" area, which served for homework and for the creation of Dungeons and Dragons games (probably what is being created here).

The Loft

 A view of the attic, aka the loft, which shows the Pilgrims Progress painting which used to hang on the landing of my grandparents' house in Oundle, but which I inherited after my Grandpa's death, and came to me when my Grandma moved to Croydon. I didn't really have anywhere for it and agreed with my Dad's suggestion that it should be donated to our local church, to hang on the wall there, which was done. Below, my sister with some of the cuddly toys who were relegated to the loft as we grew up, but never forgotten. These two survive today.

WEBS AND SHADOWS: STRANGE STORIES OF BARSETSHIRE

Paul Leone

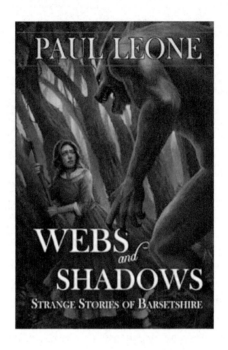

In a quiet corner of England lies the county of Barsetshire, nestled between Somerset and Wiltshire. This rural landscape is of little note to the average Briton today, who sees little more than woodlands and fields, and not the strangeness that lurks beneath. In the shadows of the Lobwold and the back alleys of Barchester, mystery abounds if you know where... and how... to look.

Webs and Shadows pulls back the curtain on the hidden history of Barsetshire, from the aftermath of the Ice Age to the end of the second Elizabethan Age, and contains nine weird tales set in 'the edge of nowhere.' Pierce the webs and cast light into the shadows as you tread the secret paths of Barsetshire between the First and Final Champions of the British Isles.

Available Now: **https://www.amazon.com/dp/B0C9S7PJ5Q/**

The Kingdom

Ciaran McLarnon

Hector was on the other side of the river, hidden by the dense foliage that skirted the banks. He was perched on a low branch of a tree that had trunk wider than he was, and Hector was an imposing figure. He was described as husky, more powerful than overweight, and sported a black beard that was wispy in places. He wore a beard because shaving seemed unnecessary and inconvenient on a long sea voyage, and when he had reached their destination it seemed even more unnecessary. He was short in stature, Hector thought it was this that gave him more agility than anyone expected. The livid white scar running just below his left eye made him look tough. He told everyone he got the scar in bar fight but told no-one he'd slipped on a paving stone while running away when he still thought he could.

Hector, sturdy as an ox, fleet as a fox, a scout beyond compare, was running again; but this time he was being followed. By a gangly youth, perhaps a few years before he gained the weight of adulthood. The youth was hunkered at a bend in the stream, where a clay embankment had been worn by animal generations into a watering place. The youth slathered copious amounts of the river water on his face, arms, and legs before drinking a little from his cupped hands.

The youth had perhaps lived in this jungle his whole life and it showed. He was comfortable enough to wear no more than he had to; only a loincloth was thought necessary here. He carried little with him, he was probably close to his village. Hector couldn't see it, but he thought the thick undergrowth of this endless forest could hide an entire village. His wiry frame and sparse clothing were like most of the local people, but many of the ways in which he behaved were different. The differences were subtle, most people perhaps wouldn't notice, but Hector had a knack for seeing veils for what they were. The boy hid the truth well for his age, but he held back something of himself. Perhaps it was the slow and careful way that he drank, Hector could easily recognise someone else who didn't fully trust the river and drank only to fulfil a basic need. Where Hector went, he gladly followed, humming and whistling his songs when the birds stopped theirs. Hector had travelled the world and had witnessed the almost universal attraction of community; someone happy to be alone was a rare and confident figure.

'New Spain will bring new riches to our kingdom and vast wealth to our king, but first that kingdom must be tamed and free from tyranny,' the captain of Hector's ship had said, 'this is what we must do our to bring the king's glory to new lands.' Hector would have preferred to stay with his wife rather than undertake this treacherous voyage, but she would understand.

There had been 5 galleons in their fleet, packed with supplies for the fledgling communities to the west. The waters were calm when they left Spain, but once they had left the Mediterranean, the swells of the Atlantic made their ships like toys, fragile things at the mercy of untamed nature. But the ocean voyage was the price of New Spain; Hector would endure. There were many days when he saw nothing but unbroken sky and ocean; he thought that witnessing such enormity might split his mind in two. When he was able to see land on the horizon again, it gave him such a spring in his step that he felt he could jump over the side of the boat from the centre of the deck.

He'd heard stories of what he could expect in New Spain, but what he had pictured bore no relation to the reality. The stories had painted a vast land of unlimited wonder, where great cities floated on water, of gargantuan pyramids that stretched towards the heavens, and of course of places where gold was in such abundance that even the streets were paved with it. This new world was indeed vast, he could see the coast on the horizon for days before his was the first ship to drop anchor in that sheltered bay. This land was a world apart from the manicured gardens and terraces he had pictured; it was a place where the land did not seem to have been sculpted by true civilisation. This was a land that seemed to lack any kind of order, where jungle spilled over the margins between land and sea, where dense undergrowth prevented any view of the interior's secrets.

He wished that he had not been so enthusiastic to join the rowboat crew for their expedition in their search for a good place to make a camp; a staging post where they could hold supplies before marching onwards into the interior. But it had been months since he had been able to go anywhere, to do anything but look at the whales and wandering birds with envy. Hector felt his urge to explore keenly, he might have jumped at any chance to be anywhere else.

As the dinghy travelled from ship to shore, he spent as much time looking through the crystal-clear waters of the tranquil bay as he did the land he was approaching. He could see the bottom easily, allowing him to gauge when he would jump. The beach was steep, the opportunity to jump came late to Hector. The water was chest high as he pushed himself away from the boat, ducking under the water and feeling all his stress fade to nothing. His enthusiasm was rewarded was with thousand tiny cuts to his feet as they sought firm ground to bear his weight. The coral was intricate and delicate, a boon for pristine waters, but the chalky spines and hard edges punctured his soft flesh with ease. Everywhere he looked Hector could see examples of this kind of sly malevolence, in this land discovery seemed to bring many pleasant surprises, but soon became unpleasant. Hector grumbled that he missed Cadiz, that for once he yearned for the familiarity he had so often tried to be free from.

The captain of his ship admitted that he also had a small measure of home sickness when he said, 'I too long for Cadiz,' but he had more to say to Hector on the matter, 'but we have all been asked to undertake this voyage to perform a duty for Spain. I have guided this ship across the ocean and am free to dream of our return. But your duties have not yet begun, you have an important role in unravelling the mysteries of these lands.'

Unravelling these mysteries would be the key to bringing the order and civility of Spain. There was an air of tranquility in a society formed around the word of Christ, without spreading his words and faith bringing enlightened thinking to these lands would be impossible. Here it was hot, it was wet, it was chaos. Hector had no doubt then that the barbarous edges to the many stories were the truest parts.

The beach he landed on consisted of white sand and added calm to the wild fringes of the forest. But he would ignore this tranquility and bring order and mastery to this land, to bring to pass those things that nature attempted to subvert with every plant that grew as it pleased, every insect that crawled and bit, with every animal that did not yet no man as a special kind of danger. He kissed the cross he carried on a necklace and offered a silent prayer after he had pleaded for protection. His scouting partner was a few steps ahead, but already almost obscured by the thick undergrowth.

'I think the howls are coming from those monkeys,' said his scouting partner, Juan. He was pointing to dark figures perched on the tree branches, bobbing their heads to look in every direction, but paying particular attention to the strangers eyeing them from the forest floor, 'I don't think we need to be wary of them.'

'Perhaps not,' said Hector, 'but perhaps something is making them nervous, so we must be careful.'

'I think maybe it us who are making them nervous,' laughed Juan, 'and listen to the birds also, they wouldn't produce such rich and complicated songs to warn of danger.'

'Who can say for sure? This world is wrong in many ways; perhaps those birds are guiding a greater danger to us.'

As they travelled further into the forest the noise changed, but it never stopped. The calls from the animals in the trees changed, the tones became higher; birds sang but perhaps not the same varieties. In wetter places frogs and toads belched, in the trees the primates held court. Everywhere ants crawled across their boots as they busily surveyed the forest floor.

A man mimicked a bird call, booming more loudly than a bird's little lungs could ever achieve. Juan and Hector both spun round. The man appeared in an instant, it was clear he had been tracking them and had chosen this moment to reveal himself. The scouts looked at each other, in silence expressing their incredulity at being tricked in such way.

'We have failed,' said Hector to his companion, who nodded his head to recognise this was true, 'but God will provide a way to redeem ourselves.'

At that moment they heard another bird song in front of them, then turned around to see another man blocking their path. Then another man appeared to the left, and another to the right; soon they were surrounded. Ahead of them, the warrior screamed as he raised his axe above his head. He charged forward and buried the blade in Juan's skull. Hector swung wildly as he dropped to the ground, cutting several men before he ran off into the forest. In the thick foliage of the forest Hector was lost within minutes; he understood how the hunters had remained invisible for so long. Soon he felt he could hide and catch his breath.

He found a moment of respite when he rested in a nook between the roots of an ancient tree with a trunk as hard as iron. He listened for signs of his pursuer's whereabouts, quickly learning the subtle differences between genuine bird song and the chatter between one tribesman and another. Sometimes they would use language that was too rapid for Hector to place, he supposed it must be their native tongue. But he was surprised that any man would speak to another in that way; even the very sounds of this language seemed unnatural to him.

To speak in this way must be a burden to these people, thought Hector, Spanish is a superior language, they will be glad to benefit from it.

The voices became more distant, Hector found the confidence to move away from his knotted sanctuary. He slowly crawled up an embankment behind him, hoping that he could remain unseen as he moved towards a better view of his surroundings. He thought he saw movements in the distance; the hunters used axes and fearsome clubs to beat heavy undergrowth as they searched for him, working with the rhythm and order of a practiced farm labourers gathering wheat.

Hector found comfort in watching these honed manoeuvres, he had so many of his own, but the fantastic and bizarre plants that surrounded him were enough to restore his tension. Giant waxy leaves and a multitude of flowers growing from every tree trunk, every space for life occupied and jealously defended. Even the insects of these forests, each bigger than Hector's thumb and a constant irritation, didn't seem to affect his pursuers. It was as if they could communicate with the insects and warn them to keep their distance.

He noticed one at the back of the group was remaining silent. He appeared to somewhat younger than the rest, a youth on the brink of maturity. He moved more slowly and with less confidence, he was at turns ignored and berated by the others. He was treated like an animal where Hector could see no others. As the light began to fade the rest of the group left that part of the jungle. The youth continued his search, those who seemed oldest shouted and pointed as they left.

Soon the forest was covered by the blue-grey light of dusk, and then the dark night crept over, but this was a land that never slept. That night the clawing heat and humidity didn't relent, moths continued to drift from flower to flower while the chirps and hisses of lizards reverberated through the forest. Hector couldn't sleep. He imagined he was in the eye of a storm. In the small clearing where he was resting, he saw a temporary peace and tranquillity, but all that he heard reminded that this peace could quickly turn to chaos, a chaos he had no power to avoid. He closed his eyes and tried to get some kind of rest, but he couldn't forget the fear that those hunting for him could be lying in wait just yards away.

True sleep was impossible, but Hector was sure he managed to doze a few times during the night. Nevertheless, when dawn's early light began to play on his eyelids, he was ready to face the challenges that the day would bring with a steel and determination thought would make his countrymen proud. Today he would begin anew, that land did not contain anything that could strike fear into a heart that belonged to his European home.

He looked around, looking for signs his pursuers. He found the youth easily enough, but all signs seemed to indicate that he was alone. He never looked over his shoulder never gave an indication that he was trying to maintain contact with anybody else. He didn't appear to be taking anyone else's orders, and most telling was that he seemed happy and at ease to make his own route.

That certainly a nice situation for a person to be in, thought Hector.

Over the next few hours, Hector began to see it as a game, a test for this young man. Wherever Hector went the youth was sure to follow. Hector never stopped moving, he thought that he went back on himself but wasn't sure. Every now and then the youth would allow Hector to hide within the thick vegetation, giving him the opportunity to observe his tracker. The youth always stayed close, but not too close. It was clear he had been given he wanted to keep a watchful eye on Hector but to engage him in any way.

That's sensible, thought Hector, I must seem very strange to him, and he wants to see how I behave before they decide what to do with me.

Hector tried to absorb as much detail about the youth as he could from his vantage point above on the opposite side of the stream. This was part of the game between the pair, it was clear that the tracker enjoyed being seen, and Hector wondered why this was.

Perhaps the youth has put some thought into his method, perhaps he hopes that the knowledge I am being followed, no matter what I do, will add to my fatigue.

Sometimes it was hard to identify a gap in the leaf cover that would give him the space needed, but Hector was able to console himself with the thought that if he was struggling to find gap then he didn't need to worry so much about being watched.

But he was always able to find a space without too much movement, always able to find a way to be content with his observation. He found the appearance of the youth completely fascinating; he was taller than his compatriots, didn't share their rounded features. His nose and chin were the sharp features with which Hector was more familiar. The other men in his group seemed to have straight hair, but the wavy hair of the youth was more akin to the types that were more familiar to Hector.

As Hector studied the youth, he could recognize more of himself than he hoped; so much so that he even began to fear he was losing his memory of civilization. He had experienced these sensations in many of the wilder places he had visited; he was always mindful of how quickly those gifts could be forgotten when a person was so far away from their source. Hector began to ponder an idea; perhaps giving this young man an experience of civilisation would be enough to allow him to benefit from a more civilised outlook on his life. Until that moment the game had been directionless, the path treaded by Hector was circuitous and vague. But now Hector had a duty to be a saviour, to lead the youth to the light. He would lead him back to the ship's crew. Hector was close to the bank, surely if he followed the river downstream, he would find himself at the coast, and therefore closer to his crew.

The novice stopped, rested on dark wood log, and picked his teeth with a twig. Hector smiled, thinking that following him downstream for hours had been more effort than the youth bargained for. He didn't show it, but Hector knew the youth must be feeling the same strain he was. Hector wasn't exactly sure where he was, his innate sense of direction told him that all he would have to do was follow the course of the river and it would guide him to the bay and the fleet of galleons. The river had to join the sea at that bay, even this strange land, where nothing was quite what it seemed, had to follow that rule.

Nevertheless, Hector's heart skipped a beat when he first heard the roar of the ocean. He did have to climb a tree above the thickest of the undergrowth to hear it, but that confirmation that he might soon be free of the jungle, that he was steering the pursuit to an end, gave him an inner strength he never knew he had. He imagined his arrival in that familiar haven; he would soon camp for the evening, and he was sure he would dream of that greater respite. He had done something to help the expedition that would bravely follow him into the unknown, and the youth who had pursued him through the jungle. The Spanish soldiers who had sent him on this mission needed guidance through this maddening forest, and the tracker behind him needed perhaps more important guidance of a spiritual kind. His follower was a primitive man, but Hector could see enough humanity in him to see that he was worthy of assistance. He smiled as he could offer the man - from the wild forest to the sanity of civilised Spain.

Hector's dreams, once so tangible and so inevitable, became childish fairy tales in an instant of inattention. Following a trail of collapsed earth had been a mistake, but the allure of a familiar trail of dirt within this alien landscape had been irresistible to him. He cursed the errant vine that tripped him, causing him to spill forward and catch his face on a jagged tree-trunk. He was dazed but unhurt. Though, when he had shaken off his stupor, he realised that he could no longer hear the Sea. This is a clever form of torture, thought Hector, always changing my surroundings so that I never become comfortable; every misstep is compounded.

Hector desperately needed a good place to sit down. But he couldn't find a good place, so he just sat down. He guessed the driest place would be against a tree, but he could only tolerate all the tiny creatures crawling over him and biting him for about a minute. He jumped up screamed, frantically brushings his arms. Hector realised his head was bobbing all around him, just like the monkeys he had seen earlier. The tribesman, where-ever he was, couldn't be seeing this and considering the scout a threat to his people. Hector could never have predicted the jungle would turn into a swamp, hopefully at its coastal fringe. He had to go there; the sea was his only target now. Hector found himself navigating towards that hellish place where worlds collide, half-way between land and water. He took some comfort from seeing that he was still being followed, at least that tribesman showed no hesitancy in following him there and following him there.

The swamp was the deepest part of his nightmare, a place where the most unpleasant facets of the Jungle, a final assault on the senses before finally released him from its grip.

Exhausted by the heat and humidity, harassed by thorns and flies, still he battled against the mud that sucked and pulled at his feet. Every step forward became a feat of strength, his legs strained to be released from the mud with every step forward. He tired quickly and soon reached the point when he could continue forward no longer. He lost his rhythm; he was sinking to the realisation that this folly could be his last. He was stuck fast, feeling himself sink further into the mud, ready to be consumed by nature and her lengthening shadows. In that moment he thought of his company and what little he had done for them; he did the unthinkable and called out to his foe.

'Help!' Hector thought this was stupid thing to call to a man who didn't know his language. Any word or sound would do, although at that moment he could think of no other and had to express his only thought.

Slowly the youth appeared from the undergrowth, pushing leaves and branches aside to make space for himself. He was unhurried, still relaxed about being seen by Hector, climbing through the trees seemed merely to be a way of avoiding the noxious sludge that festered between the gangly tree roots. As he carefully moved between the overhanging branches the tracker rarely cast his gaze upon anything but Hector for several minutes, his hard eyes trying to burrow into Hector's soul. Hector responded likewise, he doubted that his stare had the same effect on the stranger. Hector knew he looked pathetic to the youth; even though he was a novice he still had enough wit to avoid becoming embroiled in the mud.

Hector called out again, 'help,' trying to reinforce the message of his pleading eyes.

The youth stared at Hector for moment longer, wrinkling his forehead and then tilting his head from side to side, eventually offering him a stick to hold on to. He pulled Hector free from the clawing mud. Hector's carelessness had embarrassed him and made him show weakness to his foe; he was a child who got into trouble playing in the mud.

Hector managed a weak smile when the novice fell backwards. He pulled Hector towards the trees and a surer footing, then the youth lost his own. But he regained it quickly, using with the twigs and green branches of the tightly packed trees. The dappled light that had broken through the leaves fell on the stranger's face; Hector thought the youth was in camouflage as he pulled himself up to the low-hanging boughs. Hector spread his open palms to the man and stood away from him as he spoke,

'Thank-you,' Hector bowed slightly to the tribesman, 'you have saved my life and I mean to do the same would for you.'

The young man tilted his head and looked towards Hector with a blank expression. But Hector's confidence was growing, he was sure that on some level the youth could understand the spirit of his words. Hector gave him a gift, a simple wooden cross he tied around his neck with string, to emphasise his point.

'This is the light, this is the son of god that will enrich your people,' said Hector, 'all you must do is follow his teachings and believe in him.'

'God?' The man smiled as Hector handed him the gift, then beckoned Hector to follow him.

I must follow him, thought Hector. I am lost, and this man has just saved my life. I must be ready for what may come.

The man glided through the trees, within minutes they had left the swamp and were in the thick of the jungle, again. Without civilised knowledge the youth could only lead him to hell.

The two men passed through the trees in silence, almost like strangers; the space between them was filled with the patter of heavy raindrops smacking against leaves. The youth never looked back as they travelled for the rest of the day, until he stopped beside fallen tree. His eyes tracked the movements of Hector until Hector reached the clearing.

'Adan,' said the youth as he pointed to his chest, 'Adan.'

Hector pointed to the man as he replied, 'Adan.' Like Adam but not quite, thought Hector.

This clearing was where the two men would camp for the night. It was too hot for a fire and Hector seized the opportunity to take off some of his extra layers, his tunic and his boots. He noticed Adan looking curiously at them, so he offered him the clothes to examine more closely. Hector also produced his knife, and it was in this that he seemed most interested. The youth held the knife up to the moonlight creeping through the canopy, glinting off the blade and in his eye. The youth had probably seen similar tools in his tribe, but naturally they would be less sophisticated, thought Hector.

As Adan tried on the clothes Hector was again reminded that this man could pass unnoticed in any area of Spain; he could pass along cobbled streets lit by fractured sunlight, drinking, and relaxing with friends in Tavernas as he passed a sweet evening. The idea started to form.

Hector shook his head, as if he was trying to free himself from an unseen grip. But the idea stuck, he dreamed of what Adnan could be in a different place.

He awoke. In the first few seconds of disorientation Hector was not afraid. He saw something that could only be Spanish, he wondered when he'd arrived back in the camp of his countrymen. Then the maddening cries and clinging forest closed in on him, he was still within the deepest realms of the devil's trickery. Adan, the once not-quite-Adam who was now not-quite-Hector, danced and posed to complete his mockery.

Hector scrambled into the darkness of the unknown forest while Adan was still dancing and parading along the fallen tree. He didn't know how long he could survive in the jungle alone, perhaps the devil would catch him in another form, but Adan would not be the one.

For hours he struggled through the around the forest. When Hector arrived back in the clearing Adan was still there, sitting on the fallen tree in shining steel armour, picking his teeth. Hector's face dropped as Adan continued to relax, only raising his eyes for a moment to recognise the soldiers coming into the clearing. Hector's company greeted Adan as if was an old friend.

'Where is he?' Hector's captain said to Adan.

Adan barely raised his eyes as he pointed directly at Hector.

The captain smiled at this as he gave his fine steel sword to Adan.

'This man has been following me for days.' Said Hector, pointing at Adnan. 'Why do you know him?'

'If men are to be successful in any place they need friends,' replied the captain, 'And those who can keep them on the right path.' He put his hand on Adnan's shoulder, 'Adnan's tribe was the first tribe to be encountered in Hew Spain, the first friendly tribe at least. Without their help a colony might not have been established. They taught us to survive gathered us to the land we would find favourable. Their actions made them the enemies of less welcoming tribes; they were attacked, and Adnan was taken prisoner. Now he keeps his tribe alive in secret; the tribe that you saw him with a few days ago where his captors. When the time is right, we will see to it that he can get revenge, but for now he can guide our scouts back to us when they have lost their way.'

'We can reward him in another way,' said Hector, 'would it not be better that Adnan returns to Spain and helps to spread the word of our conquest?'

Adnan was sitting on his log, listing carefully to the conversation frowning at the mention of his name.

The captain grinned the at this suggestion, 'we've had our deal with Adnan for several years, and he has declined a visit to Spain. This is his home with inspite his troubles he has no wish to leave. Adnan is happy to play games with his enemies and see how it ends. In time he will be a king in this land, a leader of men. He gives old Spain an anchor that will allow our civilisation and our humanity to spread through the grateful peoples of the new.'

Ciaran LcLarnon

Ciaran McLarnon is an author from Northern Ireland. His other published works can be viewed at

ciaranjmclarnon.blog.

Details of his novel New Shores are also available through this site.

On The Trail

Matthew Spence

They were over the Ohio Crossing and already well into Eastern Virginia. Aaron Cousin, the young clay cropper who'd volunteered out of about a dozen other young men back in his native Steubenville, sat in the saddle car as he kept a dutiful watchful eye on the trees and surrounding fields with his goggles, which he'd set at close range magnification. His partner and overseer, Charles Grant, the former cavalry captain who had picked him to be his pointer, used an old-fashioned stereo 'scope that had longer magnification, but was more limited in enhancements. Grant rode the auto horse, which whirred and hissed with clockwork precision, steam venting from its hindquarters and nostrils as it trod along before it suddenly stopped, swiveling its head in a circular arc.

"What is it?" Aaron asked, keeping his voice low. "Osage?"

Grant shook his head. At nearly twice his age, Aaron thought of him as the "old man" of their expedition, but there was nothing elderly about Grant's reflexes or decision-making. "They don't come this far East this time of year. It'd be either Delaware or Pawnee here, but I'm not seeing any trail signs. No, it's something else..." Grant took a pair of earphones out of his long coat and hooked them up to the horse's head, frowning as he adjusted the head's volume controls. "It sounds like hissing," he said. "Boy, get out of the saddle car, slowly, while I dismount-and have your rifle ready. Is it charged?"

"Yes, sir," Aaron whispered back. It was a long gun, designed to hold a full battery charge for up to a day. Aaron carefully drew it out of its holster as they both knelt down behind the horse, which had taken up a defensive combat-ready position on the ground. Its head was aimed at the trees, and Aaron could see the muzzles of two mini-cannons already protruding from its "nostrils."

Kill cats, Aaron thought. They didn't have any back in the Valley territory, where the Ohio

Company had cleaned them out a generation ago. Aaron had only seen old prints of them himself, but he knew that they were big, intelligent, and liked to attack in groups of threes with one of them acting as a lookout.

The two cats came out of the woods then, saber teeth bared and claws extended. They hissed as the horse turned its head in their direction; they were obviously familiar with armored auto steeds. Grant triggered the mini-cannons while Aaron fired a lightning burst at the first cat. The second charged, but the cannons cut it down in mid-stride while Aaron judged the range of the third cat and fired again, hearing a deathly squeal as it fell out of one of the trees, dead.

"We shouldn't see any more of them on the Trail, but let's take turns keeping watch until we make it to Croatoan," Grant said. "We can warn the tribal police there, and they can wire the Commonwealth Patrol Headquarters."

"I didn't think there were any this far north," Aaron said as they resumed riding.

"Their migration patterns were disrupted during the Southern War," Grant replied. "I can recall having to deal with packs down in the Arkansas Confederacy. They must be getting hungry, too, they usually only attack at night."

By the time they crossed the mountains the Trail was straightening out as they passed through more farmland, most of it cooperatives. Crop breeders and migrant French workers were already beginning their early summer harvests as they rode past. The breeders were friendly enough, the French workers, some of whom still had bitter memories from the War, less so, although they had no real trouble with them.

By the time they reached Roanoke the farmlands had been replaced by steam plants, electric rail lines, and other property owned mostly by Edison and Atlantic Rail. Technically speaking the Trail ran through Roanoke on its way to its historical origin point in Columbia, although there were few visible traces of it in the city itself. Grant got them rooms at a hotel near the main railroad terminal that was part of the Dominion line while Aaron stabled the horse and hooked it up to the stable's charging terminal for the night.

They were awakened shortly after midnight by clanging bells and the more distant wailing of air horns. "What is it?" Aaron said as he turned the lights on, seeing them flicker and briefly fade as he did so. "Tornado?" He knew it was that time of year, although in this part of the state they were more prone to hurricanes.

Grant shook his head. "Sky's clear." Turning on the small wave radio beside his bed, they both heard a recorded announcement advising residents to seek shelter. Grant tried the tuner and found it to be playing on most of the local channels, although the state channels were playing music. "I've heard this before, during the War," Grant said. "We'd best get down to the stables. We'll be safer there than up here where we'd be exposed..."

"Exposed to what?" Aaron asked as they left the room.

"Been paying attention to the news lately?" Grant said. "Remember the problems we've been having with the Spanish down in the Gulf?"

Aaron's eyes widened. "But that would mean..."

Grant nodded. "It's come at last, son-the war fears have become fact. We are probably seeing the first wave of an airship raid-"

But even as he spoke, the building shook with the impact of more distant explosions. It was war after all, then, Aaron thought. The Commonwealth would respond, of course, and hopefully when they did there wouldn't be any more direct attacks on the mainland, but until then...

They spent the rest of the night in the stable, the horse on standby. Through the stable's narrow windows they could see the lights of fires that had been started by incendiary bombs. Of course, the Commonwealth wasn't totally unprepared, they did have coastal guns and their own airships to give chase to the enemy. But it would take time for that to happen. Until then, their small trade mission would have to wait. Aaron wondered if it would even be possible now, or if the company would be called up for action.

"Was it like this during the War?" Aaron asked. "The uncertainty, I mean."

"There were times when it felt that way," Grant admitted. "But we'll live through this. Come what may, we'll prevail."

Aaron nodded. His own father had been a scout trooper during the Southern War and had rarely talked about it. He wondered if he might become like him after all-his youth ended early, a way of life changed if not ended.

Aaron hoped not. But things would change, he was certain of that. But, as Grant had said, he would prevail.

Matthew Spence

Matthew Spence was born in Cleveland, Ohio. His work has most recently appeared in Suburban Witchcraft.

Richard Douglas Gough (1797-1886)

Part 1 – Birth to 1842

Family Background

Richard Douglas Gough was the youngest child of the Reverend Fleming Gough, who in 1796 had succeeded his uncle. James Gough Aubrey, as Rector of Cilybebyll, Glamorgan and Rector of Ystradgynlais, Breconshire, and who in 1808 succeeded his brother, Richard Gough Aubrey (second of that name) as Squire of Ynyscedwyn, Ystradgynlais.

Reverend Fleming Gough had entered the clergy in 1780 as a deacon at Saint Briavels, Gloucs, in 1782 had been at Steeple Ashton as curate, and had married Martha Taylor at Cirencester, whilst a curate in Cheriton. He had clearly moved to Glamorgan by 1787 when he was admitted to the Freemasons at the Gnoll Lodge, Neath, and in 1788 his eldest daughter, Harriet, was baptised at Margam, with a second daughter, Susannah baptised there in 1790.

It is not certain, but quite possible, that Fleming took up a curacy there, before later definitely becoming curate of Saint Mary's Church, Briton Ferry, by 1792. Whilst at Briton Ferry he would baptise his eldest son, William Fleming Gough, in September of that year aged 3 months, and then probably preside at the child's burial at the age of three and a half years in January 1796, whilst in March 1793 also bury his mother, Christiana Gough, widow of his father, William Gough junior, who had died during the Seven Years War, as a Royal Navy captain, at Quebec in 1760, whilst Fleming himself was just a small child.

The baptism of Richard Gough is recorded at Saint Mary's, Briton Ferry, on January 28th 1798, with Richard's date of birth given as 31st September 1797. This seemingly obvious fact was belied by two things - that his middle name was not part of his baptismal name, and that his age at death was three years younger, making him appear to have been born in 1800. Initially., it might be assumed that this Richard, son of Fleming and Martha Gough, is an interloper, an infant who died young, and then the name was reused for Richard Douglas Gough. But not only is their neither a burial for this presumed Richard Gough, there is not another baptism for Richard Douglas Gough.

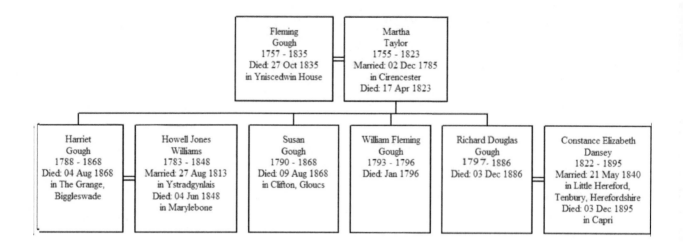

Education

When we look at the records of his education, at Harrow School, and then at Exeter College, Oxford, we find that the evidence of his age shows that the 1797 date of birth is true, and that he did indeed manage to lose three years off his age in later life.

We can see in newspapers of the time that Richard Douglas Gough is reported as graduating Exeter College, University of Oxford, in November 1820.

From the "New Times [London]" Tuesday 28 November 1820

UNIVERSITY INTELLIGENCE

Oxford, Nov 25…. Yesterday in a Congregation, the following Degrees were conferrred:-

Master of Arts - Rev Philip Laurent, St. Alban Hall, and Rev George Evans, Christ Church

Bachelor of Arts – Thos. Stratton Codrington, Esq., Brasenose College, Grand Compounder; Wm. Holled Hughes, Lincoln College; Wm. Stanhope Cole. Worcester College; Theodore Bouwens, Merton College; Robert Anstice, Wadham College; Richard Douglas Gough, Exeter College; …

We can then find in their records that he is listed as having matriculated (started his course) in 1817, aged 19. Further proof of this latter comes from a search of the college's archives (thank you to Victoria Northridge, Archivist and Records Manager) where we learn that

"He was tutored by John Collier Jones and took various classes - a variety of Greek Philosophy and Theology in the terms as follows:

Michaelmas 1817 Thucydides
Lent 1818 Theology B III
Easter 1818 Pindar
Lent 1819 Theology BVI"

They also note that he had previously been at Harrow School. Thanks to Bethany at Harrow's archive, we learn that his entry is thus:

Gough, Richard Douglas *(Mr. W. Drury's),* son of the Rev. P. Gough, Yniscedwin, Glamorgan. Admitted between Summer Term 1814 and Autumn term 1815; left 1815-16. Exeter Coll. Oxf., B.A. 1820; of Yniscedwin; J.P. Brecon and Glamorgan (High Sheriff, 1840). DIED 1886.

and that Mr. W. Drury would have been his House Master, meaning he boarded in Moretons House, which still exists today.

The key information, from Victoria Northridge, is

" Having checked the printed register by Boase, the record for Richard Douglas Gough confirms that he matriculated into Exeter College on the 28th March 1817, age 19"

Thus, we can say he attended Harrow from age 16, then Exeter College from age 19, and graduated aged 22. At this point, his age is the same as his baptismal record.

Family Matters

Richard's sister Harriet Gough married Howell Jones Williams on 27th August 1813, when she was 25. They would have four sons and four daughters, the eldest son being Walter Jones Williams (1814-1866) who would later become the Rector of Ystradgynlais from 1846 to 1856, the second son being Fleming Gough Williams, born April 1817 and died December 1817 aged 8 months, the third son being Fleming Gough Howell Games Williams, born in 1826 and who would rise quickly in the military before his death in April 1851, and the younger son being John Wilkins Williams, born in August 1832, when Harriet was 42. The daughters were Anne Harriet, born in November 1815 (and who would marry pioneering Welsh photographer Calvert Richard Jones in 1837), Susan Beata born 1820, Mary Martha Gough Williams born 1821 and Gladys Games Portrey Williams, born in early 1829.

The abundance of family names is noticeable, as is the fact that the two eldest children were baptised, presumably for a second time, by Reverend Fleming Gough himself in January 1819, and the five younger children christened in Ystradgynlais in 1834 by the curate, Timothy Davies, after being baptised elsewhere soon after birth. Given that Richard, Harriet's only brother, and Reverend Fleming Gough's only [surviving] son, did not marry until 1840, 5 years after his father's death, it is quite possible that Fleming Gough was looking to an eventual prospective succession to his lands by Harriet's family in this period.

Richard's aunt, Anne Harriet Gough (born in 1754 and sister to his father) died on 12th February 1821, unmarried, with her place of death given as Yniscedwin House, though she is recorded on the grave as having been living at Briton Ferry.. She is remembered on the gravestone in Saint Cynog's Church, Ystradgynlais where she is buried.

Richard's mother, Martha, died on April 17th 1823 and was buried in the churchyard of Ystradgynlais Parish church (at that time, the name Saint Cynog's was not remembered, nor revived). Of the Gough graves which can be seen today in a long section hers is the third chronologicallty after her brother-in-law, Richard Gough Aubrey's, and her husband's aunt, Harriet.

Horse Racing

A useful document for piecing together more of Richard Douglas Gough's life before the death of his father in 1835, is the last and will and testament of the latter, which makes clear Reverend Fleming Gough's disgust for his son's lifestyle.

Accessible at the National Archives Discovery website, Fleming Gough's will has the reference, upon download, of PROB/1860/268. Wills written up to 1858 for Southern England and most of Wales, where the deceased held property in more than one county, had to be proved by the Perogative Court of Canterbury. The Reverend Fleming Gough's will was proved at London on 20th April 1836 before the Judge by the Oath of Susan Gough, Spinster, the daughter and the sole Executrix.

On the surface, this looks strange, since his son, Richard Douglas Gough, was alive and one of the main inheritors. But the text of the will makes it quite clear why Reverend Fleming Gough chose his daughter to be executor (executrix as the female version of the word)

- - - - - - -

In the Name of Almighty God and in the hope of his mercy through the merits and mediation of my Saviour and Redeemer Jesus Christ, I Fleming Gough of Yniscedwin, Rector of Ystradgynlais, being of sound mind but infirm in body from age do make this my last Will and Testament, written with my own hand.

My Real Property and estate of Yniscedwin will of course descend to my Son and legal heir Richard Douglas Gough but as I have much reason to fear that his propensity to horseracing and gambling (a species of insanity) may devote that property to sudden destruction I have no choice left but to give and bequeath to my dear daughters Harriet Williams and Susan Gough the whole of my Personal Property of every sort and kind whatsoever, save and except such silver plate as may be in my possession at my death having armorial bearings of any kind engraved thereon, which are to descend to him the said R D Gough as heir looms.

I give and bequeath to my Grandson Walter J Williams all my Books, manuscripts and mechanical and philosophical instruments and implements save and except twenty volumes to be selected by my said daughter Susan Gough for her own use from the Books so devised.

That my intentions may not be mistaken or misconstrued be it clearly understood that as the Yniscedwin Estate will descend to my Son R D Gough. I leave him accountable to God and his Country for the management and disposal of it, only observing that if the truly Royal income of the late Duke of York was dissipated in horseracing and gambling, leaving him at last a lamentable bankrupt, what can a private Gentleman expect from indulging in such ruinous Propensities.

All my Personal property consisting of money due to me deposited in Banks arising from sale of valuation of live and dead stock and of every kind and denomination that can come under the description of title of personal property, except as before excepted, I give and bequeath to my daughters Harriet Williams and Susan Gough to be equally divided between them for their own separate use or the money arising from the same being sold to be so divided on a just and fair estimate by a competent sworn appraiser by them jointly appointed or otherwise by agreement for the estimated produce of such a Sale entered into by joint concurrence between them and their Brother R D Gough, who as my heir is to pay my debts and funeral expences which I will to be as moderate as consists with decency.

And I hereby constitute and appoint my daughter Susan Gough sole Executor of this my last Will and Testament In Witness whereof I have hereunto set my hand and seal this twenty third day of August 1831 F Gough (LS) Signed declared and published as and for his last Will and Testament in the presence of us - William Rice – John Lewis – Samuel Hal

(Additional punctuation by the Editor, to make easier sense for the reader)

In addition, Richard Douglas Gough's own obituary carried in the Bury and Norwich Post, Tuesday 14 December 1886, near to where his second home would be in his later years, records, in part:-

DEATH OF R.D. GOUGH ESQUIRE

We cut the following obituary notice from the Swansea *Cambrian*.

To those who can carry their memories back about fifty years, when horse-racing of no mean order formed one of the institutions and annual pleasures of the inhabitants of Swansea; and when the Crymlin Burrows could show at least on two days of each year such good sport as attracted horses nof repute from a distance, the name of young Gough (his father being then alive), was honourably connected with the active patronage of the turf, and with the names of the winning horses, all trained by him at Ynyscedwyn; and during the race week, his local popularity was amply vouched for by the many spontaneous ecxlamations of "Gough for ever!" that met one on every side.

Issue 4 of The Red Dragon magazine, coined the national magazine of Wales, was published in July-December 1883, edited by Charles Wilkins. One of its many articles is on the annual meeting of the Swansea Valley Archaeological Society who decided to take a perambulation around the Ystradgynlais area to look at things of historical interesting, including this passage

> "Passing onwards, the members of the society arrived at the farm of "Bryn-y-groes" or "the Hill of the Cross", the property of Mr Richard Douglas Gough, of Yniscedyn House, well-known about half a century ago for his famous stud of race-horses, and as one of the first equestrians in the Principality"

One would take "first" here to mean "leading" rather than "original".

Politics and The Law

Richard's father, Reverend Fleming Gough, died on October 27 1835, and managed to presage his son's later "problems" with age, albeit in reverse, by being somewhat older on his tombstone than he could possibly have been from his date of baptism.

In the Cardiff and Merthyr Guardian, and the Glamorgan, Monmouth and Brecon Gazette of Saturday 25 February 1837 Richard Douglas Gough's name appears among the "Additional List of the Supporters of Colonel Wood, M.P."
T. Williams of Aberpergwm is 5th on the list, and Richard Douglas Gough of some unusual spelling of Ynyscedwyn is 8th, on a list that descends to the bottom of the page.
Thomas Wood was the Conservative M.P. for Brecknockshire between 1806 and 1847

That the local Squire and landowner would be both a Conservative supporter and an Anglican was more or less a given at this time. One might presume that Richard Douglas Gough believed in the tradition and place in society he had inherited, and that he thought progress away from this was wrong, or at the very least was against his own interests.

Richard Douglas Gough became a Justice of the Peace (J.P.) for Breconshire in 1837

Cardiff and Merthyr Guardian

Glamorgan, Monmouth and Brecon Gazette

Saturday 8th July 1837

> Brecon - The Summer Assize for this county will be held on Wednesday the 26th inst, and for Radnorshire at Presteigne on Tuesday, August 2nd, before Mr Baron Gurney.

> At the late Quarter Sessions, Richard Douglas Gough of Yniscedwin, Esq.; John Jeffreys Wilkins of Maesderwen, Esq.; Charles Whire of Aberannell, Esq.; Richard Turner Roberts, of Llwynderw, Esquire; and William Davys Harries, of Noyadd, Esq., were qualified to act as Justices of the Peace for the County of Brecon

Bell's New Weekly Messenger

Sunday 18 November 1838

From the London Gazette

The names of those who were nominated for Sherrifs by the Lords of the Council, at the Exchequer, on the Morrow of St. Martin, in the Second Year of the Reign of Queen Victoria, and in the Year of our Lord, 1838

Breconshire - John Lloyd, Dinas, esq.; Howel Jones Williams, Coity, esq; Richard Douglas Gough, Yniscedwin, esq.

The website for High Sheriffs, highsheriffs.com, explains that in the November of the preceding year 3 names are suggested and that the monarch then pricks the one they want with a bodkin – now in March, but presumably in the early/mid 19th century in late January, according to the newspaper reports on actual selection.

Thus, Richard Douglas Gough would have been suggested ib 1838 for 1839 but it was John Lloyd of Dinas who was selected and who served as High Sheriff in 1839. Richard Douglas Gough, and 2 others, one assumes, would have been suggested in November 1839, and this time he was selected and chosen in January 1840 to take up the appointment of High Sheriff in the March of that year.

In 1840, Richard Douglas Gough became High Sherrif of Brecknockshire, something which his uncle, Richard Gough Aubrey had previously attained some three-plus decades before.

The London Gazette

31 January 1840

WALES

Anglesey - Sir Love Parry Jones Parry, of Madryn, Knt.

Breconshire - Richard Douglas Gough, of Yniscedwin, Esq.

The Era

Sunday 2nd February 1840

SHERIFFS APPOINTED BY HER MAJESTY IN COUNCIL FOR THE YEAR 1840

The following list of Sheriffs appeared in Friday evening's Gazette

...

WALES

Anglesey: Sir Love Parry Jones Parrhy, of Madryn, Knt.

Breconshire: Richard Douglas Gough, of Yniscedwin, Esq.

Cardiganshire: John William Lewis, of Llanarchayron, Esq.

etc

Monmouthshire Merlin

15th February 1840

SHERRIFS NOMINATED FOR 1840

Monmouthshire	Summers Harford, of Sirhowy, Esq.
Herefordshire	J. heywood, of Hope Enf, Esq.
Somersetshire	J Jarrett, of Camerton, Esq
WALES	
Breconshire	R D Gough, of Yniscedwin, Esq.
Cardiganshire	J.W. Lewis, of Llanarchayron, Esq.

It would seem that the new High Sheriffs took office from 25 March (Lady Day), the first day of the year in England and Wales under the old calendar.

William Hibbs Bevan, of Glannan succeded Richard Douglas Gough as High Sheriff in 1841 but in 1842 the third of the 1838 nominees finally attained the position, in the person of Howell Jones Williams, of Coity, who was of course Richard's brother-in-law due to his marriage to his sister Harriet.

An interesting event happened in July 1840 when Glyntawe (Callwen) was transferred from Devynock to Ystradgynlais.

Silurian

Saturday 18th July 1840

COPY OF A STATEMENT

Transmitted to the Clerk of the Peace for the

COUNTY OF BRECON

BRECONSHIRE TO WIT - To JOHN POWELL, Esq., Clerk of the Peace for the County of Brecon

"WE, FREDERICK FREDRICKS Esquire, and the Reverend DAVID HANMER GRIFFITH, Clerk, two of her Majesty's Justices of the Peace, acting in and for the said County of Brecon, do hereby give you Notice, that, in the opinion of us the said Justices, the Hamlet of Glyntawy, in the Parish of Devynock, in the said County of Brecon, ought to be annexed to the present existing Division of Ystradgunlais, in the said County, and the places within the same would form together a more proper and convenient Division within and for which Special Sessions should henceforward be held than the the Hundred of Devynock, in the said County of Brecon, of which the said Hamlet of Glyntawy forms part.

"And we do hereby further give you Notice that no other Division of the said County, save and except the said Division of Ystradgunlais and the Hundred of Devynock, will be alterd by such proposed change of the said Hamlet of Glyntawy from the Hundred of Devynock to the said Division of Ystradgunlais. And that we, the undersigned Frederick Fredricks and David Hanmer Griffith, together with Howel Gwyn, Richard Douglas Gough, Esquires, and the Reverend Charles Mayberry, Clerk, are, at the date of this statement usually resident or acting as Justices of the Peace for the said County within the Boundaries of the said proposed altered Division of Ystradgunlais. And we make this statement in pursuance and by virtue of an Act of Parliament made and passed in the ninth year of the reign of his late Majesty King George Fourth, intituled "An Act for the better regulation of Divisions in the several Counties of England and Wales."

Dated this Twenty-fourth day of June, in the year of our Lord One Thousand Eight Hundred and Forty.

 "F. FREDRICKS

 "D.H. GRIFFTH."

One of Richard Douglas Gough's duties as High Sheriff was to oversee the assizes and to call them into session.

Silurian

Saturday 1st August 1840

BRECONSHIRE

SUMMER ASSIZES 1840

I do hereby give Notice and Proclaim that the ASSIZES for the County of Brecon, will be held before the Right Honourable THOMAS ERSKINE, one of the Justices of Her Majesty's Court of Common Pleas at Westminster, on Saturday the 8th day of August next, at the SHIRE-HALL, in BRECON, when and where all Prosecutors and Witnesses bound over to Prosecute and give Evidence are required to attend, or their Recognizances will be forfeited, and when and where the Grand and Petit Jurors, and all Justices of the Peace, Mayors, Coroners, Escheators, Stewards, and also all Chief Constables and Bailiffs of every Hundreed and Liberty within my said County are required to attend, and be then and there in their proper persons, with their Rolls, Records, Indictments, and other Remembrances, to do and perform such things as shall be enjoined them or as belonging to their respective offices to be done.

Dated this 23rd day of July 1840

RICHARD DOUGLAS GOUGH

HIGH-SHERIFF

N.B. The Magistrates' Clerks are to deliver to the Clerk of the Assizes, upon the opening of the Commission, the Depositions in each case with the Recognizances of the Prosecutors and Witnesses put together.

The SHERIFF'S ORDINARY will be at the CASTLE HOTEL, on the day of opening the Commission.

Dinner on the table precisely at three o'clock.

Interestingly, Richard Douglas Gough was elected a Member of the Royal Agricultural Society in 1842, reported in the Hereford Times due to his link to that county through his marriage into the Danseys.

Hereford Times

Saturday 22nd January 1842

ROYAL AGRICULTURAL SOCIETY OF ENGLAND

The following gentlemen were elected Members of the Society:-

The Rev. Henry lisset, Letton, Herefordshire; Henry Eustatius Strickland, Apperley Court, Tewkesbury, Gloucestershire; Arthur Armitage, Moraston, near Ross, Herefordshire; Thomas Lawford junior, Peterstone Court, near Brecon, South Wales; Richard Douglas Gough (High Sherrif of Brecknockshire), Yniscedwin, Brecknockshire.

Marriage and Children

Richard Douglas Gough married Constance Elizabeth Dansey on 21 May 1840 at Little Hereford, Tenbury, Herefordshire, which was the home of the Dansey family; she was 18 and he was 42, though in later years after he had dropped 3 years somewhere along the way it would appear that he had been 39.

Constance Elizabeth Dansey was the youngest daughter of Dansey Richard Dansey, eldest son of Richard Dansey, and thus controller of the Dansey estates. Constance had 3 elder brothers and 2 elder sisters.

Leicester Herald

Saturday 13 June 1840

> On the 21st ult, at Little Hereford, Richard Douglas Gough, Esq., of Yniscedwin House, Breconshire, high sheriff of that county, to Constance Elizabeth, youngest daughter of D.R. Dansey, Esq., of Easton Court, near Ludlow

Interestingly, the birth of their first child is recorded less than a full 9 months from the date of their marriage.

New Court Gazette

Saturday 6 March 1841

BIRTHS

> On Saturday, the 27th of February, the Lady of Richard Douglas Gough, Esq., of Yniskedwin, in the county of Brecon, of a daughter

This was France Martha Gough, who would be included in the census of that year, taken on June 6th 1841, where she is correctly listed as 3 months old.

Sadly she would die in April 1842, but that was not known then of course.

Hereford Journal

4 May 1842

> April 30, at Ludlow, at her grandfather's, D. R. Dansey, Martha, daughter of
> R.D. Gough, Esq., of Ynrserdwin [sic] House, Breconshire, aged 14 months.

The memorial gravestone to Frances Martha Gough in the churchyard of Saint Cynog's Church, Ystradgynlais, incorrectly gives her age at death as 11 months, instead of the correct 14. Given she was buried at Little Hereford, there may have been some delay before this stone was created, or it could be simply a mason's error.

By then, Constance was already pregnant with their second child, another daughter:

Hereford Times

Saturday 10th September 1842

LOCAL NEWS

Births

Aug 26 at Yniscedwyn House, the lady of R.D. Gough, Esq., of a daughter

This was Constance Gwenllian Harriet Gough, and she would live well into adulthood.

The 1841 Census

The United Kingdom Census of 1841 recorded the occupants of every United Kingdom household on the night of Sunday 6 June 1841. The enactment of the Population Act 1840 meant a new procedure was adopted for taking the 1841 census. It was described as the "first modern census" as it was the first to record information about every member of the household, and administered as a single event, under central control, rather than being devolved to a local level. [Wikipedia]

This census MIGHT appear to be where Richard Douglas Gough began to lose years of his age, but it was also one where the enumerators were SUPPOSED to round down. But the rounding down of his age to 40 might have "stuck" and from then on he may have been 3 years younger than he really was.

Ynyscedwyn House

Richard Douglas Gough	40	Head
Constance Elizabeth Gough	19	
Frances Martha Gough	3 months	
Howell Jones Williams	50	
Walter Jones Williams	25	
Calvert Richard Jones	35	Clergyman
Anne Harriet Jones	25	
Christiana HVG Jones	2	
Maria Elizabeth Powell	20	
Anne Wilkes	35	Servant of 1 (i.e. Richard Douglas Gough)
Jessie James	25	as above (female)
Mary Yapp	25	
Mary Seabourn	30	
Anne Davies	15	

Anne Jones	30	
Sarah Stocke	20	
Thomas Rees	20	as above (male)
Robert Whitefoot	30	
James Thomas	15	
George Roderick	14	

Thank you to people on Twitter for vetting the original photocopies of the names, and coming up with the above, especially for the servants who by-and-large are not attested elsewhere, except for Jessie James, who has a plaque in Saint Cynog's Church, Ystradgynlais.

In addition to Richard Douglas Gough, his wife Constance, and at this period their only child, the census shows extended family members present on the night of June 6th 1841.

Thus we have Howell Jones Williams, the husband of Richard's sister Harriet, who is not present, which is interesting. Howell and Harriet's son Walter Jones Williams is present, as is their daughter Anne Harriet, who was married to the Rector of Loughor, Calvert Richard Jones, who was also an important Welsh pioneer in the field of photography. Their young daughter Christiana is also recorded aged 2, with her middle names abbreviated to the letters H.V.G.

Richard Calvert Jones had become Rector of Loughor on 19th May 1829. Anne Harriet was born in 1815 as the second [surviving] child, and eldest daughter of her parents. She married him on 24 July 1837 at Ystradgynlais. As such she was the niece of Richard Douglas Gough, and their child Christiana Henrietta Victoria Games Jones was his great-niece.

I have yet to identify who Maria Elizabeth Powell, aged 20, is. She appears above the list of servants of Richard Douglas Gough, implying she is a visitor, but it is possible she is a governess or some such brought by Calvert Richard Jones and Anne Harriet.

Fair-Weather Friend: Part 2

Mark Harbinger

IV.

Ulm, Bavaria—1735, Anno Domini.

"Erains! Erains! Tell us another story!" the children bellowed at him. They gathered 'round their favorite raconteur with rapt attention.

"I want to be with her her every day, out in the sunshine!" Erains declared to the crowd.

'Her' was the fair maiden Agnet. Agnet was daughter to the town smithy, and officially promised to another, Tomas, a brutish oaf whom she wanted no part of. Tomas would beat her if she so much as looked at anyone else. And Agnet's father had made it clear to the Reverend that he expected Erains to stay away from his daughter.

He had no recourse but to comply. As personal assistant to Superintendent Von Sand, he was expected to stay out of the personal lives of the congregation members.

Thus, he would steal into the tree near her window in her home at night and fling small notes of affection into her window. If they ever managed to cross paths during the day, he would quickly rush home and grab his violin. To play her a song.

There was once when they bumped into each other, outside the village limits. That was a glorious day. A Summer Day for the ages...

"What? What, sir?" the kids were puzzled.

And Erains looked at them again and realized what he had spoken aloud. A familiar warm, shame rose in his face. His waking dreams were as prevalent as ever. And while he had less time for releasing his special oils of passion as he did when he was younger, his predilection for exploring strong emotions had not abated.

Were anyone to look, he had carefully engraved into his own living flesh many of his favorite passages from scripture. This had become routine--rapturous visions and cutting his flesh; He didn't know how to explain it. The pain made him feel real, again—instead of this fantasy that he walked through every day.

"Yes. That is, while we are out here in the sunshine, let's enjoy a story, shall we?" And while the children cheered in response, he started to think about which of his own waking dreams, the ones he saw when people around him slept, he would alter and craft into a worthy tale...

Before he could begin, though, he caught a glimpse of her, back in the distance. The unmistakable hair atop the head always tilted to continue the natural curves of her body.

Agnet.

He smiled at her and when he caught her eye, she smiled back.

Whenever he thought about her, he winced inside; oh, how he wished he leave Ulm with her, to take her back to the place from whence he had come. But he knew that wasn't possible. For either of them.

She was promised to another.

And he had responsibilities, too.

Erains had impressed the Reverend with his various talents over the years. Erains especially benefitted the older minister by guiding him as to which subject that week's sermon should be about. He didn't tell Master Von Sand that he was actually peering into the future, with the help of the Holy Ones, to see what the good reverend was going to cover. But, Church attendance had never been higher. And everyone thought well of young Erains. So, the Master, too, found him in favor.

"Children, turn around and see that pretty lady?" he shouted loud enough for her to hear. "Now, sing it just as I taught you! Go on! One, two, three...As sure as the weather...!"

"*As sure as the weather, is a lover's heaaaart*," they all sang to her, while she clapped her hands in delight and listened.

Ser Erains was so pleased with himself that he didn't even notice the large black and brown carriage approaching behind him.

The children aborted their song as the carriage parked alongside.

A tall, slender man emerged from the carriage. He wore the regalia of an officer of King Frederick's royal guard. It was the same outfit that the Crown Prince had worn five years before, except now he filled it out. He was different. Much more confident and imposing in stance, yet the look in his eyes was unmistakable: Crown Prince Frederick II had returned.

"You there! I am told you are Ser Erains?" he bellowed at the younger man.

"I am."

"Yes, I recognize you now. Well met. Come with me. We have business to discuss." And he placed his hand on Erains's shoulder, to remove any decision.

The children all scurried away as Erains looked over his shoulder. Agnet's face was concerned. She started to come forward to take issue, but Erains subtly waved her away.

Frederick, however, picked up on it and nodded to his driver.

"Ah, yes. Her, too. This concerns her, as well."

When the driver pulled her to them by the arm, Frederick noticed the bracelet upon her wrist.

"My goodness. You must be quite the special lady to deserve such a gift." he said to her with a touch of scorn. "Right, then. Bring her."

"What happened? you ask. Well, let's see," Frederick began, with a wince, "My overconfidence in the plan was my undoing. Not two weeks after you and I met, my father captured Officer Katte and myself, threatened us both with charges of Treason, and ultimately...settled...upon merely beheading Goodman Katte— killing him, right before my eyes—so as to avoid the embarrassment of his own son being charged. I was convicted by a Court Martial, but, the Bishop decided, after a healthy payment from my father, that I was innocent because Katte was an *unholy influence* upon me. So it was agreed, *by all*." Frederick now shot a dark stare at Erains, as though talking about him. "It's funny how easily men can conjure divine inspiration, when they want to."

Agnet was seated off at a different table at the side of the room—left alone, but in earshot—while Erains just sat and stared at the despondent royal before him.

"Anyway, after that, the monarch stripped me of my rank, and released me from jail into another prison, of sorts. For two and one-half years I was in Küstrin, being trained in military strategy and tactics...a very different schooling than what I had been used to as a child. The only visions I had during those years were of a good night's sleep." He chuckled and poured himself another draught.

"However, one good emerged: It was there that I finally learned this important lesson: Tactics outvie strategy.

"For example, when faced with my own forced marriage—to the estimable Hapsburg, Lady Elisabeth Christine—I decided that, while my own suicide would no doubt have been a fine *strategic* victory, instead agreeing to the marriage in order to secure my own release from that prison-academy, and to further return to my father's good graces, was the proper *tactical* choice."

Frederick considered his libation, his grim smile partially obscured by the shadow of his brim. "That worked so well he promoted me to Colonel. I then lead a contingent of the Emperor's soldiers in the latest war over the Polish succession—but, good Erains, being a fine, simple man, I can see you are bored with all of this. Not the least of which because *you've already seen it, have you not? We both did!*" Frederick's mouth quivered, while the veins in his forehead were visible.

"So, tell me, my young prophet, what have *you* been up to?"

And while Erains carefully recounted how he had become a trusted servant to the Reverend, Frederick merely nodded, pausing only to ask about how the bracelet had or had not been used.

"I have only used it to divine the weather...to assist with the Reverend's prognostications for the veracity of his sermons. F-for some reason it works best when she and I are together." Erains truthfully said. "It has g-g-given me an excuse to hold her hand." *Before everyone forbade me to see her.*

"Ah, I'm sure you have plenty of reason to do that, Erains." Frederick smiled, already wistfully looking back to those earlier years of innocence.

"W-w-why are you here, S-sire?" Erains asked.

"Your directness does you credit. It's quite simple. You and I, and your lady friend, we all are going on a trip. To visit my father. There you can fulfill your Oath to me. We leave, on the nonce. I will explain more fully along the way."

Two days later. A small cottage inside the grounds of Hohenzollern Castle, Prussia.
"The Crown Prince wishes to see you, Your Majesty."

Frederick William I's shoulders sagged ever so slightly. While his son had accounted himself well in recent campaigns, he would ever remain a disappointment to the monarch. The King hoped and prayed that the rigors of war had finally purged his son of his sodomite ways, but deep down he was skeptical. He would likely never produce a grandson, a true heir.

"Does he have him?"

"Yes, sire."

"Very well." he waved with a gout-ridden hand, remaining at the modest table in his royal study.

"How goes the battle at Clausen, father?" the Crown Prince began, as he strode into the room, with two people, a man in a monk's robe and a young lady, at his back.

Such insolence, the King thought. "You apparently left your manners at whichever salon of recreants you last visited. You will address me as Your Majesty, especially in the presence of guests. And is it not your first duty to introduce these strangers to me, *boy?*"

The King could see Ser Erains and his lady-friend were visibly shaken to be in his presence. And disturbed he was angry. They didn't know: He was the one who had sent his son to fetch the young wizard, of course. But, this lady was a surprise. The King perked up at the thought that his son had taken an interest.

"Of course, Your Majesty. I present to you, Ser Erains, who has been surnamed Murawuns by the Good Reverend Von Sand, and his friend, maiden Agnet of Ulm."

Murawuns, the King chuckled to himself. That means '*one who mumbles*' or '*one who grumbles*' in Prussian. *A wizard who isn't well-spoken. Well, hopefully, he isn't mute. Still, this should be entertaining.*

"I welcome you both to my castle and, further, to my private cottage. My son must think highly of you, *both* of you, to allow you to accompany him." Before anyone could say anything, the King turned his attention to his son, "At Clausen. The cease fire has been arranged and couriers have been sent to inform the combatants there. But, the battle continues. The latest word was that Seckendorff had pushed forward, across the Rhine, and our forces were in retreat. I warned our French partners that getting involved in Poland's domestic squabbles was unwise. It doesn't please me to always be right."

"Truly, the burdens of your own wisdom are a weight only you can bear, Your Majesty." the younger Frederick said, with a bow and not a hint of mockery.

Impudent welp. I should have killed you with your demon-possessed companion, the King reflected.

His son continued: "I have brought the one you sought, Your Majesty. The Reverend's recommendation may...still have worth." Indeed, August Von Sand was a most trusted advisor and a *de facto* member of the King's war council; he had suggested this wizard's ability to control weather could be the key to a sudden, unexpected Winter campaign.

"So, Ser Erains, I am told that you have some skills with weather charms."

"A-ay, yes, yessire."

The King beckoned everyone to sit down with a broad smile. "Show me."

At that, The King noticed Frederick's sober facade momentarily slip into an eager grin. *Just what does he think is about to happen here?*

The other three gathered around and sat—Fritz made sure that the Erains boy was seated at the far end. *Another gesture of disrespect? Or part of the wizardry?* The King was always amazed by what the Lady Roucelle (who had helped to raise him as well, when he was young) was able to do. The tricks she showed him. The charms. Even fortune-telling.

She said that there were spirits present, but the King never felt them. But he believed she could work her little magicks. And, by all accounts, this lad was of another order higher in his abilities.

Let us see.

Fritz knew what the King wanted. The King wanted to see him control the weather, to prove he could. And, apparently, they had discussed it before—because Fritz just nodded to Erains and Erains put his hand in the middle of the table. Now the girl is, too. *Wait, she is wearing that bracelet that Roucelle gave Fritz? What is the significance?*

Glancing at Frederick, he noticed that his son was positively jubilant, a ravenous look in his eyes. The girl just looked at her lap, occasionally stealing a glance at Erains, who tried his best to give her his strength with an extra squeeze of his hand, where all three of their hands were meeting.

The King snuck a glance outside. Nothing, yet.

He just sat and stared at the three of them, waiting for something to occur.

The entire carriage ride Frederick laid out his plan for revenge to Erains. They would summon the storm together. Slay the King. Then he would see to their escape, Erains and Agnet's.

But, Erains was skeptical. In fact, the entire trip there, Erains cursed himself for his own lack of courage. If he were a man of action, the carriage trip here itself would have been precisely the chance he had been dreaming of. He should have slipped away with Agnet, unbeknownst to Frederick, and finally make their escape!

But, he had been too afraid of this tall and terrible scion seated across from him in the carriage. And Agnet was so afraid, she was shivering. He could not risk her being harmed. He was responsible for her now, he thought to himself. She had never traveled from Ulm before. She hadn't even been given the chance to say goodbye to her family.

The long walk through the palace, up so many flights of steps he had lost count. And, all that only to pass through the castle entirely, and into a small courtyard.

The courtyard contained a cottage that was a small house that the sovereign used as a private study?

He could barely focus, as the two royals bantered. He stammered an answer to the King's query. And then they all sat down and joined hands.

Erains could feel the electricity in the air. The Holy Ones were *with* them, *there,* in that place.

Erains and Frederick both saw the visions spinning past them, in the open air above the table, the future was unfolding. Scenes of an explosion of fire raining from the sky.

Erains thought he could hear Frederick's voice inside his mind: "Just as we discussed! He is a murder and tyrant. I will reward you, handsomely! You swore an Oath. See the storm you need...the one that brings the fury of the heavens and rains it upon my father's head!"

Such anger! Erains was unmoved by Frederick's exhortations; instead, he focused on his beloved Agnet, even now his heart wanted to leap from his chest to help steady her. She was so scared—*Wait, what is this?* And, then Erains saw further ahead, after the bizarre lightning strike that slays the King. *It is the Crown Prince laying upon the ground! And Agnet! Agnet is being taken away by soldiers?* And the scene quivered before him, like colors flickering sunshine passing through a waterfall. *Frederick betrays me? This is all a suicide attempt?* He can see Agnet screaming out "HELP ME!"...*No! Agnet!*

At that, Erains started to put it together...a lightning strike kills this Crown Prince while he and two strangers are visiting the king—one stranger being an unknown female. She would be tried as a witch! Of course! *No, this cannot be.*

Beyond anyone's notice, the slowly revolving dark knot of clouds far off in the distance had barely begun to twirl when Erains broke off contact. He stood up and stumbled, falling backward over his chair, the screams of Agnet still echoing in his mind.

"M-M'lord!" Erains yelped. "Y-You, I will not do this. I-I cannot."

The Crown Prince was circumspect. "What are you saying, young one?"

"My Oath was to The King. The storm you would have me summon. It-it might harm The King...I-I am sorry. I cannot do what you ask. Agnet, come! We must go. Quickly!" He stood up and help her from the table. Numbly, he leaned forward in a bow. "Thank you for your hospitality, Your Majesty. We beg your leave to return to our home."

"Of course, my young friend. You may go." And then he paused to look at his son.

"But, Agnet will stay. She will stay as concubine to Fritz, here. And, when she has given birth to a proper heir, she will be released to return home. In the meantime, you will be well taken care of. I shall see a regular delivery of gold and supplies is delivered to you and your church superintendent in Ulm. August will like that." Then he bellowed: "Biggles!"

After a few short moments, a eunuch entered from a side door in the study. A glance of recognition of the Crown Prince caused pause, but for only a moment: "Yes, Sire?"

"Biggles, take the Lady Agnet of Ulm here, and set her up as part of my son's *special* retinue."

"Of course, Sire!" And Biggles merely turned and made the smallest of gestures towards some shadows at the edge of the room.

"No!" Agnet yelled. Two soldiers grabbed her. She started to struggle, but the soldiers that had been standing by the door—*Had they been there all along?*—sprung forward to make sure Biggles needn't exert himself. They firmly took the squirming girl from the chambers. She looked over her shoulders at Erains and gave a plaintiff yell:

"Help Me!"

Just as in my vision. Erains could only stand in horror as his love was dragged from the study. *Did I do this?* Looking over at the Crown Prince, he could see that he also was at a loss. But, being a schooled player at Court, he recovered more quickly than Erains could.

"Father! Your Majesty," Frederick stood and bowed, "I take it you will allow me to gather this charlatan of a weather-wizard and take leave of you."

"Yes. And what else, my fine son?"

It took Frederick the Second a moment, but, apparently this wasn't the first time this had happened with a young girl. "And *Thank You* for yet another lovely lady for my retinue, father. Hopefully this one will be more...fecund than the rest."

"Indeed. Perhaps I'll have the vizier draw you a picture of instruction, so you can know just what to put where. Now, begone! Both of you! Before my mood takes an ugly turn at today's little disappointment and I decide to take measure of whatever unholy *oath* you two are referring to. Just please do me the favor of not holding hands again, as the two of you leave." The King poured himself a drink and, without looking up, bellowed: "Now, go!"

By now, Erains, who had avoided eye contact all along, was staring at the King, seeing him for the very first time. Frederick William's obese frame was draped in silk linens and a shiny brocade of slated leather, which dumbly reflected the candlelight in strange streaks across the room. He sat hunched over, slightly, as though weary from activity or worry. The skin of his great, cherubic head was clean-shaven, and it sat in layers—one layer of skin under the chin, which held the layer of his lips, which held up his cheeks. Another long, flat layer held back the white wig which covered his salted hair. But the final layer, in the exact center of his skull, was the flabby crescents under his eyes.

Those eyes!

Only the King's eyes betrayed his inner-fire.

The Crown Prince had told him that the King routinely beat him as a child, and would violently attack anyone who crossed him, at a moment's notice. He could see that truth of that in Frederick William's eyes.

Of course, the *Holy Ones* were there, too, in the room—Erains could sense them. They spared Erains more images of prophecy...a few years in the future, *This flabby, angry King, dead of natural causes. Frederick II taking the throne.*

Finally, a sharper image: *The two of us, Cleric Murawuns and King Frederick—standing, toe-to-toe, arguing, a duel to the death...for Agnet!*

It was murky, but Erains survives. The Holy Ones were clear on that much...

Does Frederick not see that, too?

Then the connection was severed. The Crown Prince was pulling him from the room, no doubt to have him beaten and locked up somewhere.

But, there were no beatings nor stockades. Erains hoped that Frederick would rail against him so that he could explain *I am not a killer! He is still the King, not you! I swore an oath! Kill him yourself!*

But that argument, that chance to vent, wasn't a vision of the future—only wishful thinking. Instead, there was only a defeated Crown Prince, telling his assistants to set Erains up with provisions and send him away, back to his life in Ulm.

Before they parted, Frederick did explain that Agnet would act as a personal assistant to one of the female members of the Royal Family. She would be trained in the ways of the Court.

He also made it clear that he had no intention of fathering any child with her. She would be well taken care of. But, by decree of The King, she would never be allowed to leave.

This time there was no letter. Erains would speak for himself and tell Von Sand what had happened. And it would be for Erains to tell Agnet's family that their daughter was now a lady in waiting for a Court, and a future King.

V.

It was a new day, just not for his soul. Ser Erains Murawuns kicked his legs over the side to attach them to the ground beside his hay-stuffed bedroll. Then the old man—who looked too young to make such a noise—grunted himself upright. He stood alone in the house, squinting and yawning.

Strutting out to relieve himself, he spared a glance out past the trees of the forest to the West. He could sense it coming: *Delightful!* The slight quickening of the clouds, the darkened skies, and the sudden sting of cornflowers' upon his nose. He returned to his hut and took out his violin. Time to resume his quest. *This time the song will be perfect*, he thought.

Agnet, *Sweet Agnet*, always liked his songs. She said so once, on that special Summer Day. But, each time, as the song ended, she always left the same way—with a wistful *Thank you. I must go*. Each time.

And, each time, Agnet's departure would rip Erains's heart from his very bosom, and he would feel it fall to the ground and drift away, floating down the road-side gutter, along with the last, lingering notes of the song and the mocking rainfall that had so many times failed him.

He had to face it. Never again would she be his. Not since the Mad King's intervention.

No, he closed his eyes while he played, to avert the memory—forcing even more of the elemental magicks into his playing. *This time it will be different! She will love me!*

Unlike the song before, this new song would mimic even more the notes of happier times: Sweet Agnet and him, holding hands amid the bachelor buttons of the fields. Making love under the stars of the Bavarian sky. Even crowding together, under the shelter of the trees, as lesser storms moved past.

Satisfied at this latest tune, and feeling the nascent electrical charges in the air, he doffed his cap and set out to where she would be. Every day she was always outside, in the patch of tall trees alongside the stables, on the opposite end of the village.

His heart felt heavy as he caught his first glimpse of her. She stood by herself, all alone. She held a bucket, no doubt sent on some errand to fetch something, but she paid it no mind.

As usual, he didn't wait for her attention. He just began playing.

At the first note, she turned to meet his gaze, her hair careening past her head. She placed her hands akimbo and fixed her face with an unreadable expression. She listened to this new song— the latest, most potent, living embodiment of his love. All of his passion. His fury. Even his pain.

Call and response, his melody was reflected by the change in the very air around them. The elements themselves trying to forge the alchemy of their love.

And—with the first hint of a slight sheen of moisture atop his brow—the song ended. He let the bow fall to his side, waiting for her approval.

She smiled at him and her beneficence filled his entire being with the energy of the ages. For a moment, he thought that feeling was all he would ever need.

Then her visage turned wistful. She tilted her head and gently bit her lip as though he would never understand.

"Thank you. I must go."

TO BE CONCLUDED IN PART 3 NEXT ISSUE

Mark Harbinger

Mark's writing has been featured in various online e-zines over the past twenty years. Publications in the pandemic era include: 2 stories for The Noncomformist literary website (2019, 2020); a humorous fantasy short in the 4th edition of the Running Wild Anthology of Stories (2021); self-publishing both an urban fantasy novel and an anthology comic (2021); and, most recently, his poetry has been in BlazeVOX (2022) and upcoming in Poetry Pacific (2024). A retired attorney and IT educator—Mark also directs a philanthropic foundation and enjoys being a father, husband, and a proud servant to Murray A. Goodness (the Cat).

Wrong Men

L. G. Parker

]

THE WRONG MAN,

IN THE WRONG PLACE,

AT THE WRONG TIME

Shakespeare wrote, "Some men are born great, some achieve greatness, and some have greatness thrust upon them." The converse is also true. Some people reject greatness even when it is literally handed to them. The consequences can be significant. Consider the case of two Union generals with the uncanny ability to snatch defeat from the jaws of victory.

General George B. McClellan, the "Young Napoleon"

Starting at Fort Monroe Army of the Potomac pushed to within seven miles of the Confederate White House during the Peninsula Campaign. When General Joseph E. Johnston was wounded at the Battle of Seven Pines or Fair Oaks as it was also called, Jefferson Davis appointed Robert E. Lee to command the Confederate forces protecting Richmond. General Lee ended that threat, albeit at great cost. In the Seven Days Battle (25 June - 01 July 1862) Lee drove the Union Army led by General George B. McClellan from the gates of the capital. Two months later, he soundly defeated General John Pope at the Second Battle of Manassas (29-30 August 1862). To recover after Second Manassas or Bull Run, as it was known in the south, the defeated Federal army retreated to the safety of Washington, which was heavily fortified, well stocked and strongly garrisoned (1). Encouraged by these victories, General Lee resolved to carry the war to the North. With the shattered Federal army temporarily out of action, Lee was determined to seize the opportunity for a bold strike that might change the calculus of war. Tactically an operation in Union territory would give Virginians time to bring in the harvest and recover from the ravages of successive Union campaigns in the Old

Dominion. It would also provide an opportunity for his army to provision from the bountiful farms and vast stores located in Maryland and Pennsylvania. Finally, there was the prospect of drawing recruits from the Old Line state. Historically and geographically, Maryland was part of the south; politically, its population was deeply divided regarding the War of Succession. Strategically a victory on Union soil might bring Maryland into the Confederacy, force Lincoln to negotiate peace terms or provide the impetus for England (who viewed the United States as a growing economic rival) and France (who had imperial dreams in Mexico) to recognize the Confederate States. International recognition would greatly increase the possibility of diplomatic, economic or military intervention. Any of these outcomes would significantly enhance the Southern cause.

With those objectives in mind, on 03 September 1862 the Army of Northern Virginia departed Centreville, where it had rested and refitted since the Second Battle of Manassas. As the regimental bands played *Maryland, My Maryland*, Lee's "lean and hungry wolves" as one Maryland lad described them, crossed the Potomac River above Leesburg on 07 September 1862, halting at Frederick on 10 September. With the Union Army still in disarray following the debacle at Second Manassas, Lee did not expect it to move quickly. As Lee remarked to one of his generals, "He (McClellan) is an able general but a very cautious one. His army is in a very demoralized and chaotic condition, and will not be prepared for offensive operations - or he will think so - for three or four weeks. Before that time I hope to be on the Susquehanna." Confident in his abilities and those of his undefeated army Lee divided his small force of just 38,000 men into four parts. Lee ordered General Jackson with 12,000 men to march to Williamsport, from there to Martinsburg, drive the Union garrison toward Harpers Ferry and then move up to Bolivar Heights. General McLaws with 9,000 men was detailed to march to Burkittsville and from there to descend on Maryland Heights. General Walker with 4,000 men was tasked with re-crossing the Potomac, marching up the south bank and seizing Loudoun Heights. Once in position these forces would surround and neutralize the Union garrison at Harper's Ferry thereby eliminating any threat to the army's rear and securing its supply line through the Shenandoah Valley. Lee ordered General Longstreet to take the fourth element (8,000 men) to Hagerstown to threaten Pennsylvania. Lastly, Lee moved 5,000 men, General D. H. Hill's division, from Frederick to Boonsboro to guard the passes (Turner's Gap, Fox's Gap and Crampton's Gap) through South Mountain. Although extremely dangerous in the face of superior numbers, this disposition of forces would simultaneously threaten Washington, Baltimore and Philadelphia. Furthermore, this course of action would confuse the enemy regarding his intentions. With so many objectives to protect, effective counter measures would be difficult. In addition, uncertainty breeds mistakes. An ill-advised move by his opponent might precipitate the decisive battle he sought in Federal territory.

As he had been in the Shenandoah Valley campaign (March - June 1862) Jackson was hugely successful. After a three-day siege (13-15 September 1862), Union forces capitulated. Jackson took 11,500 prisoners at Harpers Ferry securing the army's flank. More importantly, he also took 13,000 small arms, 73 cannon and supplies desperately needed by the Confederate Army. During that short period however, the military situation had changed drastically for General Lee. Learning that Lee was on the march, President Lincoln, in desperation, restored McClellan to command. It was an extremely distasteful decision for Lincoln. His cabinet members were adamantly opposed. To a man, they signed a strongly worded letter of protest detailing McClellan's unfitness for command. As Lincoln explained to his secretary John Hay however, "We must use what tools we have. There is no man in the Army who can lick these troops of ours into shape half as well as he. If he can't fight himself, he excels in making others ready to fight." In this respect, Lincoln was correct. McClellan, who was a brilliant administrator and greatly admired by the rank and file, quickly reorganized the Union army. Leaving 72,000 men under General Nathaniel P. Banks to man the fortifications of Washington, the balance of that reconstituted and reinvigorated force (approximately 85,000 men) marched from Washington to find Lee and bring him to battle. The Federal army arrived at Frederick on 13 September. There the gods of war smiled on McClellan for the 27th Indiana Volunteers pitched their tents where D. H. Hill's division had bivouacked just three days before. Among the debris of the Confederate camp Corporal Barton W. Mitchell chanced upon an envelope. Inside he found three cigars wrapped in a piece of paper. That sheet of paper was a copy of Special Orders 191, Lee's precise plan of operation. By the afternoon of 13 September, Lee's orders to his senior commanders were in McClellan's hands. Alerted to the danger by a Confederate sympathizer Lee dispatched couriers to his commanders and began to withdraw, first to South Mountain, then to Sharpsburg where his far-flung regiments were ordered to rendezvous.

Never the less, the widely scattered Confederate army was now in grave danger of defeat in detail. For at that moment, Lee had 25,000 men at Harpers Ferry, another 8,000 at Hagerstown and just 5,000 at Boonsboro. McClellan on the other hand had 65,000 men at Frederick a scant fifteen miles away and another 20,000 men readily available a few miles to the south. An elated McClellan telegraphed President Lincoln, "I have the whole rebel force in front of me, but I am confident, and no time shall be lost. I think Lee has made a gross mistake, and that he will be severely punished for it. I have the plans of the rebels, and will catch them in their own trap if my men are equal to the emergency. Will send you trophies." To his staff McClellan boasted, "Now I know what to do. Here is a paper with which if I cannot whip Bobbie Lee, I will be willing to go home."

Bellicose statements are one thing. Immediate and effective action is another. Fortunately for General Lee, McClellan's words far exceeded his deeds in the days ahead. At West Point McClellan studied the noted military theorist Baron Antoine Henri de Jomini, who had served as Chief of Staff to Marshal Michel Ney. He attended seminars on Napoleon and Frederick the Great given by Denis Hart Mahan. Posted as an observer during the Crimean War he had the opportunity to study the French and British armies in action. There is no doubt McClellan was an accomplished student of war, a superb organizer and an excellent engineer. McClellan was not however, as he vainly thought, a master of his craft. Although he was well versed in the mechanics of war and able to devise sound operational plans, McClellan lacked the ability to successfully execute those plans under the vagaries and stress of battle. Secretive, arrogant, insubordinate and cautious to the point of paranoia, McClellan habitually over estimated the strength and capabilities of his opponent and consequently acted with excessive care. His men called him the "Young Napoleon" but McClellan had never taken Bonaparte's maxims regarding rapid march, concentration of force, or leadership to heart:

Rapid march augments the morale of an army and increases the chances of victory.
A great captain supplies all deficiencies by his courage and marches boldly to meet the attack.
When you have resolved to fight a battle, collect your whole force. Dispense with nothing. A single battalion sometimes wins the day.
Strategy is the art of making use of time and space. I am less concerned about the latter than the former. Space we can recover, lost time never.
An army of lions commanded by a deer will never be an army of lions.
In war men are nothing; it is the man who is everything. The general is the head, the whole of an army. It was not the Roman army that conquered Gaul, but Caesar.

The gods of war are fickle. They gave McClellan the means to defeat Lee but not the character. If he had acted immediately, the Army of Northern Virginia could not have survived. For all his bold talk however, McClellan was psychologically incapable of bold maneuver. At a time when audacity might have saved the Union garrison at Harpers Ferry, smashed the Army of Northern Virginia and possibly ended the Civil War in the fall of 1862 McClellan delayed an incredible eighteen hours. Not until the morning of 14 September did he engage Lee's rearguard at South Mountain. Victorious there it took him another day to move on Sharpsburg only seven miles southwest and at that time garrisoned by a mere 16,000 Confederates. On 16 September, McClellan cancelled an attack due to morning fog. This further delay allowed Jackson's and Walker's men to complete their forced march from Harpers Ferry. The gift of four days from the time McClellan obtained the lost copy of Special Orders 191 to the opening volleys of the Battle of Antietam enabled Lee to recall all but one division of his widely scattered army and take up a strong position roughly following Antietam Creek and the Hagerstown Pike daring McClellan to attack. In light of McClellan's numbers, with his back to the Potomac River and Boteler's Ford his only line of retreat it was a defiant, many would argue suicidal move. For even then had McClellan used his vastly superior numbers properly, he could have overwhelmed the Army of Northern Virginia. Thus, the stage was set for the bloodiest day in American military history when about 38,000 Confederates clashed with approximately 85,000 Union soldiers.

Lee had formed the Army of Northern Virginia with Jackson on the left flank, D. H. Hill holding the center and Longstreet on the right flank. Arrayed opposite the Confederates from north to south were the forces commanded by General Hooker (I Corps), General Mansfield (XII Corps), General Sumner (II Corps) and General Burnside (IX Corps). McClellan placed all of Fitz John Porter's V Corps, all of his cavalry and most of William B. Franklin's VII Corps - a force by itself larger than the opposing Army of Northern Virginia - in reserve.

Of his plan McClellan wrote, "The design was to make the main attack upon the enemies left - at least to create a diversion in favor of the main attack, with the hope of something more, by assailing the enemies right - and, as soon as one or both of the flank movements were successful, to attack their center with any reserve I might then have in hand." Under the circumstances, it was a good plan. Had McClellan followed his "design" the Army of Northern Virginia could not have survived. Had McClellan better communicated his concept to the Corps commanders responsible for executing the operation he would have indeed "punished" Lee as he had promised Lincoln. Instead of a coordinated assault however, the attacks went in piecemeal enabling Lee to shift units from relatively quiet sections of the line to more heavily contested areas.

Blood began to spill at 0600 when Hooker sent his troops through the North Woods and Miller's Cornfield toward Jackson's lines. Mansfield followed with an assault through the East Woods at 0730. Throughout the morning the Confederates repulsed each assault and immediately counter attacked. Of that portion of the battle one Union general wrote, "In the time I am writing every stalk of corn in the northern part of the field was cut as closely as could have been done with a knife, and the slain lay in rows precisely as they had stood in ranks a few moments before." One Union division caught enfilade in the West Woods suffered 2,300 casualties in twenty minutes. General Sumner continued the assault on the Confederate left at 0900 with an attack aimed at the Dunker Church. At 1030 he switched his axis of attack to the center of the Confederate line. There the Rebels had taken up a near impregnable position along a sunken farm road. Backed by several cannon they repulsed every attack and did not yield until a misunderstood order for one unit to withdraw caused a general withdrawal. Losses were so heavy on that track it earned the name "Bloody Lane." Burnside began his attack on the Confederate right at 1000 but crippled the assault by funneling his men onto a single bridge across Antietam Creek disregarding fords above and below the span. 550 men commanded by Brigadier General Toombs entrenched on the high ground on the opposite bank were able to hold an entire Corps of 11,000 men at bay until 1300. Only when the Confederates ran low on ammunition were the Federals able to carry what to this day is known as "Burnside's Bridge." Rather than pushing the exhausted Rebels immediately, Burnside paused to bring reinforcements to the far side. When he renewed the assault at 1530, he easily drove the Confederates to the outskirts of Sharpsburg. Just when it seemed that Lee would be cut off from Boteler's Ford, his only line of retreat, and trapped against the Potomac River General A. P. Hill's division arrived on the field. The last unit to leave Harpers Ferry, exhausted from a forced march, they never the less took Burnside's men in the flank with a furious charge. Caught by surprise the Federals retreated all the way back to the stream that had cost them so much to cross. In this manner, the fighting ended on 17 September 1862. Overnight Lee shortened his lines and on the 18th dared McClellan to renew the battle but the day passed with only skirmishing between the armies. Realizing there was nothing further to be gained; Lee crossed the Potomac at Shepherdstown on 19 September returning to Virginia. McClellan still had all of Fitz John Porter's V Corps, all of his cavalry and most of William B. Franklin's VII Corps, who had not fired a shot during the battle, in reserve but declined to pursue the battered Rebel army allowing them to retreat unmolested. The Union army remained at Sharpsburg for five weeks. On 05 November 1862 an exasperated President Lincoln relieved McClellan for the second and last time replacing him with, as events would prove in December 1862, the unfortunate choice of General Ambrose Burnside. Outraged by the condemnation heaped upon him McClellan, as he had after the Peninsula campaign, accused the administration of sabotage. Even though he had outnumbered Lee by nearly three to one, he claimed, among other things, that he had been refused reinforcements. He became an increasingly bitter and vociferous critic of Lincoln. As the Democratic candidate he ran against his former Commander in Chief, the man he had on many occasions referred to as "nothing more than a well meaning baboon...a gorilla...unworthy of his high position" in the election of 1864. McClellan's mortally wounded ego aside, General Porter Alexander, an artillery officer in the Army of Northern Virginia, had the truth of it. Thirty years after the war he wrote, "The only thing that saved the Confederate army was the Good Lord's putting it into McClellan's heart to keep Fitz John Porter's corps entirely out of the battle and most of Franklin's nearly out. . . . Common sense was shouting, 'Your adversary is backed against a river, with no bridge and only one ford, and that the worst one on the whole river. If you whip him now, you destroy him utterly, root and branch and bag and baggage. Not twice in a lifetime does such a chance come to any general." At Antietam McClellan violated all the basic maxims of war - effective communication, bold maneuver, concentration of force, inspired leadership. As noted by Theodore Ayrault Dodge however, "The maxims of war are but a meaningless page to him who cannot apply them."

Except for the accounting, the Battle of Antietam was over. That accounting was horrendous. The Army of Northern Virginia suffered 1512 killed, 7816 wounded and 1844 missing or captured, a total of 11,172 casualties, thirty per cent of its strength. The Army of the Potomac lost 2108 killed, 9549 wounded and 753 missing or captured, a total of 12,410 casualties, fifteen per cent of its total force but twenty-five per cent of those actually engaged. At 23,582 casualties the Battle of Antietam was the bloodiest single day in American military history.

Tactically a draw, strategically Antietam was a Union victory. Since Lee had conceded the field, Lincoln used the opportunity to issue the Emancipation Proclamation changing the dynamic of the war.

General Joseph Hooker

John Hennessey introduces his excellent article on the first day of battle at Chancellorsville with the remarks, "War is filled with turning points large and small. Some constitute great tides of history. More of them mark subtle changes in momentum or policy that reverberate in their own way. On May 1, 1863, on often-overlooked lands east of Chancellorsville, the Civil War took one of those turns, commencing a bloody tide of events that would climax two months hence at Gettysburg."

General Joseph Hooker, fifth commander of the Army of the Potomac in just over two years, should have won the Battle of Chancellorsville. The war should have ended in the spring of 1863. Initially Hooker held all the advantages - superior numbers, superior position, the element of surprise and the initiative. He had caught Lee flat footed with a wide flanking maneuver. He held the Army of Northern Virginia in a vise, outnumbered two to one, caught between the Army of the Potomac and the forces he had left at Fredericksburg. No matter which way Lee turned his army would be taken in the rear. His reforms regarding daily rations, sanitary conditions, treatment of wounded and an improved furlough system had restored his men's confidence and morale. His army was ready to fight, eager to redeem themselves after the Union fiasco at Fredericksburg. To his troops Hooker boasted, "I have the finest army on the planet. I have the finest army the sun ever shone on. If the enemy does not run, God help them. May God have mercy on General Lee, for I will have none." At the critical moment however, the general whose aggressiveness on the battlefield had earned him the nickname "Fighting Joe Hooker" lost his nerve. Snatching defeat from the jaws of victory, Hooker surrendered all his advantages, most importantly, the initiative, to Lee. Dangerously dividing his army in the face of vastly superior numbers, Lee sent Jackson on a flanking maneuver of his own that rolled up the Union line, routing the Union right. Even at that point, Hooker could have regained the initiative for he still enjoyed superior numbers and Jackson's advance following the headlong retreat of Slocum's XII Corps had placed Sickles' III Corps and Meade's V Corps on his left. An attack on the open Confederate flank might have reversed the tide of battle. Instead Hooker withdrew. Lee's decisive victory at Chancellorsville emboldened him to attempt his second and final invasion of the North. However, the loss of Stonewall Jackson at Chancellorsville deprived Lee of his greatest Lieutenant, the one man who might have wrought a Confederate victory at Gettysburg as he had at Chancellorsville.

As for General Joseph Hooker, in a war infamous for the spectacular rise and equally dramatic fall of political generals, Hooker took the art of self-advocacy to a new level. Recklessly aggressive on the battlefield, he also aggressively used his political connections to embellish his reputation in Washington. In addition, he used those same connections to tarnish the reputations of potential rivals. Given senior command following the Union fiasco at Fredericksburg, he failed utterly. Adding insult to injury not only is his name linked with the Union debacle at Chancellorsville; it also became synonymous with those ladies of easy virtue who provided companionship at the notorious parties held by his Headquarters Staff. Captain

Charles F. Adams, Jr. (1st Massachusetts Cavalry) described Hooker's Headquarters as a cross between a "bar-room and a brothel."

Conclusion

General McClellan could have ended the Civil War in 1862. General Hooker could have ended the internecine bloodshed in 1863. Neither had the requisite personal character or martial ability to do so. Instead the war would drag on until April 1865 at a cost of thousands killed, wounded or missing, economic devastation for the former Confederacy and cultural rifts that linger to this day.

Footnotes

(1) Fortress Washington consisted of 48 mutually supporting strong points connected by earthworks and 480 heavy cannon, served by 7,200 artillerymen. At Lincoln's insistence, for he was well aware of the political significance of the nation's capital, the army also maintained a large garrison of infantry and cavalry.

The Cuckoo's Gaze

(A *Morar's Four* story)

Peter Molnár

"Stay there only as long as is necessary," pointed out Jolivet.

Denis Morar got out of the car at the gate to the grounds of a stately country home. He slammed the door and walked to the gate. The guards and security personnel escorted him to the main entrance. The entry vestibule opened into a tasteful and sumptuous meeting room. Soon, the owner of the estate in TL-2004 showed up. A tame-looking golden lion tamarin sat on his shoulder.

"Mr. Sundström?"

"Mr. Morar. Welcome. We meet in person for the first time."

"Nonetheless, as part of our cooperation thus far, I hope you've been satisfied with the services of my team."

"I can't complain! I was honestly surprised at the promptness with which you delivered those two… liberated quagga. A beautiful pair indeed. I believe we'll still manage to expand their population to a smaller herd. If it worked successfully with tarpans and kiangs, let's hope it'll work with quaggas as well."

"What'll it be this time? A thylacine? Something smaller, dodos? A great auk? I warn you, I'm not a diver, nor much of a sailor. I'm not going to chase after river dolphins or the Steller's sea cow."

Sundström smiled, amused. He handed the monkey a small piece of fruit or cooked pulp. The cute marmoset didn't hesitate twice. It took the gift in its tiny simian hands and started munching on it patiently. The owner seemed to be deep in thought for a moment, looking at the small furry creature, as if wanting to make eye contact.

"You have a sense of humour, Mr. Morar," Sundström turned to Denis after a short moment. "I appreciate it when people aren't awfully dry in attitude. Your new mission, should you accept it, will go after endemics in the central Atlantic. Just between you and me, you'll have access to a Virgin Earth timeline."

"Mr. Sundström, I consider it an honour. Truth be told, so far, I've only had the honour twice."

"Let's not waste time inside the house. Come outside. Consuella and I are having a visit from an expert guest." he nodded to Denis and headed to the door.

Denis followed him to the veranda, where Sundström's wife and a younger woman were sitting in wicker chairs. A woman in her thirties, of a similar age as Denis, dressed more formally. They stood up and Sundström introduced them to each other.

"Nice to meet you." Consuella shook his hand. "My Kalle has praised your team highly, so many times. Humble, friendly, professional. You're no loutish mercenaries, that's for sure."

"Pleased to meet you as well," said Dr. Nowicka, who had just taken off her smoky-tinted sunglasses. "Honestly, I can't say that I approve of Mr. Sundström's approach. Nevertheless, I think you're involved in a worthy cause. But all this… espionage... and these heists… it's not for me…"

"I don't hide the fact that it's not exactly the most honest... job. However, it's not just about the challenge or the money."

"Honey," Sundström addressed his wife, handing her their lion tamarin. "Will you see to Darwin for me? I want to talk to Mr. Morar alone, before we have lunch."

They were walking around the vast back yard of the mansion, only a small part of the entire complex. Although the residence looked old, it was built using a combination of techniques from historical mansions and concepts from content-related modernist currents. Some of the outer walls seemed to pass into rocks, cascades, waterfalls, or fig tree-covered facades of Buddhist temples. In the more distant corners of the area, you could see greenhouses, signs of arboretums, big game reserves, a zoo, and a breeding station.

Wind turbines were spinning at various locations of the overall area. They had a peculiar design. On the outside, it imitated some features of historical windmills, but also appeared very organic. As if carved (or artificially grown?) from the bones of giant animals or perhaps from whale bones.

"Familiar?" Kalle gestured widely with his hand towards the individual buildings. "Frank Lloyd Wright, Jørn Oberg Utzon, Lebbeus Woods... Well-known in my native TL-75. I've used my resources to fulfill their visions. The marriage of architecture with the organic, with nature."

"I don't know much about architecture. Anyway, conceptually nice and interesting."

"I appreciate what you're doing, Mr. Morar. I think people like me, well provided for until old age, carry a certain debt... I don't know. Maybe we're sentimental old fools who just have a guilty conscience and don't like paperwork. But I, Consuella, many like me, we…" he hesitated.

"You don't want to hoard, to show off. You want to protect," Denis smiled thoughtfully.

"Why do species decline faster in every timeline with overly intensive human activity? Why did even Neolithic and Bronze Age farmers deforest vast areas of Europe, the Mediterranean, Asia, parts of the Americas? Why did our ancestors, even those with Paleolithic-level technology, exterminate exemplary species of megafauna almost all over the world? Why do people in many timelines cry, lament and have regrets far too late, when the local diversity of species declines and resists any efforts to restore it?"

"Lots of rhetorical questions, Mr. Sundström. I'll admit they've often crossed my mind."

"Sometimes I think we humans impoverish ourselves so much, by impoverishing our worlds, because we couldn't tolerate even a hint of competition. Our ancestors and us had shortsightedly culled and killed anything that seemed to pose a "threat" to our imagined crown. The arrogant, self-proclaimed crown of creation," expressed Kalle.

He pulled a business card from his pocket and handed it to Denis.

"Mr. Morar, I don't want to make excessive demands, but I would like to ask you and your team to take a guest with you on this latest mission. My longtime associate and collaborator. Info on the card. If you don't like it and it rubs you the wrong way, you and your team don't have to take the assignment and I'll get back to you later. Trust me, he's a reliable person. If you trust me and my wife, you can trust him."

"I'll take you by your word, Mr. Sundström. We'll provide the fauna clients as best as possible. It's a virgin timeline, so I guess we'll make do with a calm bit of 'hiking'. A small territory, and given the nature of the endemics, it won't take us much time. And all right, we'll trust that acquaintance of yours. If you don't mind, we'll trust, but verify."

"Thank you. I'll leave it up to you. Cooperate with him, but be willing to stand up for your team."

An hour later, after having lunch together and closing the meeting, Denis got back in the car.

"Okay, Jolly," he turned to Rémy Jolivet, sitting behind the wheel. "500 metres, then wait."

"I hope she won't take too long," remarked Denis' colleague. After 500 metres, they stopped and waited.

Once a quarter of an hour had passed, Dr. Nowicka approached the car, walking with a calm step. She took off her sunglasses, opened the door and calmly got into the car. She slammed the door, exhaled.

"So how did it go, Ms doctor?," laughed Rémy. Magda Kotwicz nudged him in the shoulder. "One day, I'll get fed up with doing intel-gathering among our customers for you lot."

"My sides are splitting... these heists, this espionage," Denis drawled and chuckled. "You should've heard her, Jolly. If I didn't know you, Magdush, I'd be afraid that 'Dr. Nowicka' would start flirting with me."

"You're not my type, boss." Magda rolled her eyes with indignation. "Well, gentlemen, we can go. I don't have a good impression about Sundström's acquaintance. Let's turn to Paston to be sure."

London

Denis had to admit, seeing St. Paul's Cathedral in a predominantly Gothic style, in its more original form, wasn't a common sight in all timelines. It left an impression on him every time he visited TL-494. Together with Rémy, they walked a few streets further, to the gastropub Speedwell's. Bertram Paston was already waiting for them, lunching on fish, chips and lettuce in vinegar.

"Hello, Bert. Oh, you Englishmen, what is it with you, having a mania for fish and chips in nearly every timeline?" Rémy grinned. "Your girlfriend recommended the salad as part of your diet. Or was it a colleague?"

"We don't have a mania for fish and chips. We have a mania for polite mutterings about the weather," Bertram sarcastically retorted. "TL-42 unbreaded Alaskan pollock, great stuff," he added. "Well, Mr. Caragiale, Mr. Simenon, let's get down to business," he immediately turned serious, almost from one moment to the next, as if in an abrupt cut.

They sat down. *You really fell for it*, thought Denis. The informant placed several printed materials on the table, including a brochure of a certain company, and one or two photos of an unknown man in his fifties.

"I already know from you that Sundström mentioned to you a certain collaborator whom he trusts. He should probably be more careful. Why? That supposedly reliable pal of his has several suspicious circumstances in his in-depth biography. Dissemination of classified information, probable attempt to penetrate the classified archives of the IDA and Indimpol. My sources and I are not sure of his real name. He operates under the cover name Svätopluk Papučka."

"Wait, *Papučka*?! Slipper?! You've got to be kidding me..." Denis sputtered.

"He still needs to work on his pseudonyms," Rémy chuckled calmly.

"Years ago, in TL-75 in that timeline's Germany, he founded a cross-timeline transport company called Schmetterling Verkehr. Outwardly transparent, at least from a legal point of view. Not a shell company case. However! There are indications that not everything about its activities is exactly kosher. For example, evidence has emerged that in the more marginal section of the company's operations, both the accounting documentation of income and expenditure, and the documentation of imports and exports, are deliberately distorted to some extent. Specifically, the company was to transport medical equipment to some little-known customers, directly to their home timelines. On paper, the service appears to have been properly performed, but my IDA colleague and I found clear indication that the tech delivery was not headed for its destination. And this was just medical technology. It doesn't end there. We suspect that Papučka's SV essentially smuggled construction and development technology, including energy equipment and commercial vehicle parts, into an unknown timeline. Even weapons, at least to a small extent. Papučka, or whatever he's called, doesn't have a completely clear conscience."

"Smugglers are absolutely revolting," Denis scowled, though he had an urge to smile at the irony of his statement. "Sundström is a good soul, but maybe he got involved with someone unscrupulous. Butterfly Transport, Slipper, would you get a load of those names and titles..."

"For a long time now, there've been rumors about Sundström's connections with smugglers. So far, his participation in the so-called collector smuggling, or, if you will, 'rescue' smuggling of extinct species, has not been proven. 'Rescue', pshaw..." noted Paston. "I'm glad you're on my side and ours, gentlemen."

"With pleasure," Rémy said, smiling as he did. Paston moved the individual documentation across the table.

"Bert, you know very well that we care a great deal about exposing smugglers," said Denis innocently.

"Schmetterling Verkehr." Magda was examining the documentation about Papučka's company. "Butterfly wing flaps, and without them, there would be no timelines, no me, no you, no history," she hummed almost thoughtfully.

"Where to now, boss?" asked Rémy. "Should we start preparing the gear?"

"Yes. In addition, you'll arrange transport with these portal-handlers," he handed the address to Magda. "In the meantime, I'll head over to TL-37 for a day or two and try to catch a flight to Korea there. She may hesitate even more than last time, but I believe I'll be convincing."

Busan

Chae-won Hwangbo was washing and disinfecting her hands. Today was an exhausting day. She couldn't wait to leave the laboratory and the institute. The cloak, overalls and protective elements have already been put aside in the dressing room, but the protocol required consistent hand washing even after the work clothes were placed in storage. She dried and wiped her hands, turned to the exit. She froze. Denis Morar stood there.

"Hi, Chae," he said, slightly embarrassed. "I'm sorry we haven't seen each other for quite a while."

She looked at him in disbelief, then with an immediately narky look.

"You?" she sighed with an annoyed undertone. "What brought you here this time, you damned Romanian..."

"*Nu, nu, doamnă,*" in his native language, he imitated the phrase of a certain detective figure. "Not Romanian, but Moldovan!" he smiled, pretending outrage. "Please remember it."

"You can be a door-to-door salesman bigwig from Ruritania, for all I care, but if you've come here to reel me back into your illegal escapades, kindly chuck that idea out of your head. And if you're here for personal reasons, forget it. It's over, Denis. You know that full well."

"What about your research, Chae-won? Are you still involved in that project to establish a reservation for species at risk of the genetic weakening of their populations?"

"I'm working on it, yes," she wiped her face in a tired manner. "The development's slower right now, but promising. Satisfied with this answer?"

"Perfectly. Without reservation."

"Excellent. Because I'm not interested in any offer. Once was more than enough. And don't forget that I've helped you and your people several times before."

"Chae, to cut to the chase: I appreciate every pinch of help that you've given me and my team in recent years. And that's exactly why I want to give you an offer. It's clear to me that project could use more funding. I've worked in science, I know there are no researchers who earn a fortune."

"Den, it's a generous offer, but understand one thing. I can't be bought. I have my principles."

"I swear, I don't want to buy your participation in the next mission of my team, I..."

"What do you want then?" she asked in a matter-of-factly tone. A tired smile appeared on her face. "You're not much of a liar, man. Tell me with complete sincerity that you need a genetics expert for the job. Someone who can handle work not only in the lab, but also in the field. Yes, the additional finances for the project would be welcome. But..."

"At least it's obvious I only like intelligent women who don't allow others to boss them around."

"Flattery will get you nowhere." she grinned.

They got off the tram and headed to a public park. The conversation flowed in various directions.

"You've never told me before where your interest emerged. You're a graduated zoologist."

"When I was in elementary school, we learned about state symbols of countries, including ours. I asked the teacher why Moldova has a bull in its coat of arms. She replied that it's not a bull, but an aurochs. The original wild cattle of Europe. I asked her where you could see one. She grew more serious and revealed that, unfortunately, the last ones were extirpated already in the 17th century. An ancestor of domestic cattle, it hasn't been present in our nature for half a millennium. Exterminated not only in my native P-264, or your P-37, but in so many other timelines as well."

"Let me guess. That experience had sparked your interest in extinct and endangered species."

"We all start somewhere when we get excited for science in our childhoods. What's your anamnesis?"

"That'd make for a longer story," a mild smile appeared on her face. He finally had the impression she was no longer as annoyed with him as before.

"If it was possible to return the aurochs to the wild, I'd support it without hesitation."

"Why isn't the smuggling only about the DNA of the species, only the male and female sex cells? More practical. "

"Guess," he looked at her, and then he looked forward, walking slowly by her side.

"Hmm… instincts, behaviour. Environment. Say you revive, e.g. a species dead for half a millennium, and then what? Where will it live? Who do you choose as its surrogate parent, not only to give birth to it, but also to raise it? How and from whom will a de-extinct specimen learn to be an aurochs, a mammoth, a dodo, etc.," pondered Chae-won.

"Exactly," Denis said. His voice was calm, almost contemplative. "After the initial wave of enthusiasm for smuggling biomaterial for *in vitro* gamete creation, there came a sobering realization, and the enthusiasm died down. This is why me and the team focus more on smuggling living individuals. Ideally in pairs."

"That Sundström will have his work cut out for him until he collects enough couples from each of the surveyed species," she replied. "Den, I'm really tired. Listen, wait until tomorrow. I'll tell you my decision in the morning."

"I'm staying at a cheap hotel. I'll wait. Until then, perhaps I'll manage to decipher the hangul on my accomodation bill."

Cape Town

In a secret underground complex, Rémy Jolivet was examining the research and hiking equipment and modest armament for the upcoming mission. He was doing the final check-up on the condition of his scoped air-powered dartgun and two small submachine guns reminiscent of overgrown pistols, when his three colleagues entered the room.

Chae-won waved at him, with a somewhat sour smile on her face.

"So he convinced you." Rémy giggled charitably. "Denis, show her respect. She's a rare person."

"Quite a modest loadout. Don't you have at least a few bullets that can travel back in time?" jabbed Denis.

"I have a sufficient number of soporific doses for our feathered clients. Should be enough, accounting for their size," explained Rémy. "Chae, we'll have no network connection there, but I've procured maps of the island, both physical ones and digital ones for the tablet. Maybe there won't be a 100 % match in everything, but the terrain is similar."

"Ah, here you are," Nkosazana Bhule, the head of the local team, welcomed them at the headquarters of the compound. She was in her early forties, and had many years of experience in providing secret cross-timeline transport as a local illegal portal-handler. "Mr. Morar, it's been a long time since you've used the services of my colleagues," she smiled happily. "I'm pleased to see all four of you here. There'll be five of you soon. Sundström contacted me. His acquaintance will arrive here in a moment, he's meant to join your mission."

"Speak of the devil," said an older male voice. They turned around. A man, somewhere between the age of fifty and sixty, entered the headquarters. "Ms Bhule. Mr. Morar? Pleased to meet you."

He traded handshakes with both of them.

"Svätopluk Papučka, I presume?" asked Denis.

The man smiled.

"It's just a cover name. If it's all right with you, I'd like to talk with your entire team alone.

Would you be willing?" he looked at Morar, then Bhule.

They nodded.

Chae felt uneasy.

The doors were closed behind them, in a small office with glass doors. They looked at the temporary member of the team.

"First of all, my name is Kováč. Aurel Kováč. I've been occasionally working with Kalle Sundström, for a fair few years now. He trusts me. And I feel honored that you've equally decided to trust me."

"Mr. Kováč, we're glad that you're willing to talk to us openly, in this manner. I have a question: Why a Virgin Earth timeline? Rather prestigious, and simultaneously, risky. You know very well that the IDA pays extra attention to any attempts at infiltrating timelines of that type, especially due to their rarity."

"True. I don't deny it's risky. The individual species from the island sought by Mr. Sundström simply occur there only in a small number of timelines. We have no choice in this."

A few hours remained until their departure. Chae overheard Denis' voice and a lively conversation in the common room. She found him sitting at the table along with Mateusz, a portal technician, and Mandil, a zoologist and zookeeper. She knocked on the doorframe.
"Hope I'm not disturbing, guys?"
"Not at all, Chae! Grab a chair," Denis nodded merrily and drank a sip of tea. "We're just talking about our line of work. Also about how they have rather authoritarian governments in Mateusz's timeline. Ones that aren't too fond of even legally approved reintroduction of extinct species."
"Mateusz and Denis like the idea of reintroducing the aurochs into the wilderness of several timelines. A suitable environment's the first prerequisite, that much is obvious, but you also need a surrogate mother for the creature, and parents for the basic education of a species' newborn. Personally, I think the most viable option in this case are wild yaks. Evolutionarily and genetically closest to the aurochs."

The portal was revving up, the transport membrane forming.
"I hope you won't accidentally throw us into the past, or wherever," remarked Chae half-jokingly.
"Time travel is impossible," Bhule grinned. "The past would be rewritten or it would simply cause chaos, and the future hasn't happened yet. Cross-timeline travel is probably the closest alternative. Since you're travelling to a Virgin Earth timeline, the exit point is unstable. It'd be a stable point if we had the relevant portal infrastructure built over there. Once you're on the other side, we'll have to put the connection into snooze mode to reduce energy expenses. Even in snooze mode, they're really huge," explained Bhule, enjoying Chae's curiosity and nervousness.
"Don't tell us any break-a-leg wishes," said Kováč. "Even without them, it'll be a physically demanding excursion."
"In a rare exception, we'll not adhere to 'ladies go first'," quipped Denis and walked forward. He was followed by Kováč, then Rémy. Chae went fourth, a little uneasy, and the group was closed out by Magda. Chae hesitated for a second. She closed her eyes, took a deep breath and stepped forward into the portal. She didn't experience any describable sensations. There were no sounds, patterns, dazzling lights or energies… There was neither darkness nor a mist. There was only the vague perception of movement. Then the space in front of her started to illuminate, become wavy...

Saint Helena

Chae stepped onto the stony beach in the north of the island. Nearby, the surf washed against the rocky coast.
"Welcome to the middle of the Atlantic," announced Denis in his affable voice.
She felt malaise, but still smiled.

For a moment, she shielded her eyes with her hand, her eyes adjusting to the sunny weather. Temperatures were similar to subtropical ones, there were various little clouds in the sky, it didn't look like rain. Her eyes wandered on the rocky cliffsides of the valley in front of them. A valley going uphill, headed for a greener interior. Their route. She was starting to feel a bit dizzy, but she took one more look back at the portal through which they had arrived. It was a narrow formation of an approximately lens-like shape. Optically completely transparent, but it rippled like air above a campfire.

She noticed Rémy as he went to the portal and said something into a modified radio. A short moment later, the ripples ceased to be so distinctive, becoming barely visible.

"That's that. Time to go."

The malaise overwhelmed her. Denis quickly walked over to her and helped her sit down on a nearby rock. Magda offered her a pill against nausea and water from a canteen.

"All right?"

"Strange," opined Chae, while Magda poured water in the cap-cup of the canteen. "Whenever I traveled between timelines on other occassions, I didn't experience such nausea."

"Maybe it's the impact of a journey ending with an unstable point of the portal."

A few minutes later, she started feeling better again. They decided to go as soon as possible. They had about sixteen hours of time.

"Dammit, I've probably caught a pebble in my shoe," Kováč muttered. "Go. I'll catch up with you right away."

The climb up the valley, where Jamestown, Cidade de João, or other alternate small towns would exist in many different timelines, was quite boring. The five of them felt more relaxed once they began approaching the edges of the inland forest. Rémy suddenly waved his hand, gesturing them to halt. He unslung the air rifle from his shoulder. Denis took a look through his binoculars. A few hundred metres away from them, higher on the hill, strolled one of the flightless, endemic rails of the island. Rémy held his breath, squeezed the trigger. The bird, now with a tranq-dart sticking out of its body, slowly lay down, falling asleep.

"Our first specimen of *Aphanocrex podarces*. Nice shot, Jolly," said Denis.

They rested at a small forest clearing in the mountains, on the northern side of the main mountain ridge. The tree tops rustled under the pleasant but brisk breeze blowing from the coast. Next to the temporary camp stood several cases with ventilation openings and inside lining. Denis checked on a smaller case with giant earwigs, to see if they had enough plants. Kováč was observing the species they caught, including two pairs of large flightless hoopoes, two pairs of rails, and one pair of flightless pigeons resting in the larger cases. Magda sat on a tarp and studied their botanical samples of *Nesiota elliptica*, *Heliotropium pannifolium*, *Wahlenbergia roxburghii*, of the tree fern *Dicksonia arborescens*, or the bizarre trees of the *Asteraceae* family, Nearby stood a smaller folding stand equipped with solar panels, powering a whirring portable DNA sequencer, monitored closely by Chae.

"It'd be splendid if we had these conveniences commercially available in our native timelines," she said with appreciation. "Well, ladies and gentlemen, in the case of the hoopoe, we have an almost 100 % match with the patchwork genome of its equivalent from our timelines. As with the terrain of the island, it's not a complete match, but almost."

"Sundström had also mentioned this recently," noted Denis. "The rails, hoopoes and earwigs we'll transport with us from Saint Helena, may not, on an evolutionary level, entirely match those we know from my native TL-264, your TL-37, etc. It's like with that one competing group a few years ago, when they tried to smuggle a few smaller dinosaurs from one of the more exotic virgin timelines without people. The joke was on them, as these weren't the popular species from more than 65 million years ago, the sort that the *nouveau riche* type and enthusiast wants to see, but species..."

"... which continued their evolution for tens of millions of years," finished Chae, guessing.

"Yes. All of a sudden, everyone was disappointed that many flightless specimens were much more reminescent of actual birds, or strange reptiles with a dense, feather-like fuzz for ice age conditions and a colder climate in the temperate and arctic climatic zones, rather than looking like everyone's idea of prehistoric monsters. Honestly, when capturing extinct critters, I prefer those from the timespan of human history, including our little "stunted dinosaurs" over here. These rails from Helena will, at most, peck us gently, rather than bite us."

An hour later they continued their trek through the mountains, towards the southern part of the island. Rémy continued regularly marking the sections of the route with a special odor spray. Most of the trails were clear enough, in regular use by the small local wildlife, but sometimes they came across obstacles while passing through parts of the mountain thicket. Rémy occassionally pulled out a machete, worn in a scabbard on his belt, and cut through the thicker parts of the vegetation that were in the way, carving out a path.

Strange, thought Chae, *to be probably the first ever people to walk through this area and modify the environment to our advantage.*

She was noticing the occassional flyby of a native cuckoo or thin, zippy dragonfly, or a dusky - black beetle with a narrower head and thinner legs.

"Would you look at these little rascals?" intoned Kováč, with a hint of surprise. He picked up one of the several yellow-coloured tiny arthropods that had crawled onto his clothes and hat. He scrutinized the little yellow 'bug'.

"Harmless," noted Magda. "The spiky yellow woodlouse, *Pseudolaureola atlantica*, if I'm not mistaken..." she explained.

"Yep," Denis walked over to them and gently brushed a few of them away from Kováč's clothes, making sure not to kill any. "They're harmless, but have a bit of a habit of crawling on people if they're wading slowly through the mountain thicket. Not bugs or other local insects. They're terrestrial crustaceans, like other species of woodlice, but also occur on shrubs and trees in addition to the forest floor."

Chae noticed one of them on her shoulder. She let it crawl onto her finger, then her palm. She rested her back and head against a nearby tree fern trunk, and examined the critter.

"Hm," she took a closer look at it. "Hello there, little fellow. This is you only home in the whole wide world, isn't it? Wonder if your DNA's largely the same as your cousins in our timelines." In a few minutes, they resumed the hike.

The terrain didn't quite match Chae's maps, but they eventually found the most traversable pass and began to slowly descend down the steep slopes. The lower part of the southern valley was slightly wetter and more forested than in the majority of other timelines. The bay at the end of the valley was known in many timelines as Sandy Bay.

They stood on the beach in the bay. They unloaded the cases with the captured animals and unpacked part of their gear.

"Mr. Morar, don't forget that obligation," said Kováč. "Survey, on that hill above the bay."

Denis nodded in agreement. He took only a few minor items and started following Kováč. When passing next to Rémy, he stopped for a moment and showed him a set of agreed-upon gestures. Jolly nodded. When both men were at a distance, Rémy waved to Magda and did another series of gestures. He picked up his air rifle and one of the submachine guns and started to secretly trail Morar and Kováč.

"Rémy followed them?" inquired Chae. Magda looked in the direction the three had gradually gone in, then leaned in to Chae's ear and whispered something to her.

"Do you really think Kováč is cooking up something against us?" replied Chae, shocked, speaking as quietly as she could.

Magda nodded.

"I'm trying to be silent because, besides Kováč, there's also another thing that's equally suspicious. Follow me," she pointed towards one corner of the bay, and started walking at a swift pace. "I've noticed it earlier. So, do you see it?"

"What exactly..." pondered Chae, her voice uncertain. Magda stopped, then pointed her finger slightly upwards, inland. At a height of about three metres, there was a very thin, approximately triangular shape, shifting shades of colours and textures wildly, and not blending in with the surroundings.

Magda walked closer, with her hands spread forward. She walked until her hands sensed... a wall. She crouched, starting to remove the wet sand of the beach with her hands. Chae ran to her and helped. A short while later, they had unearthed the edge of a metal foundation. At one particular point of the edge, there was a shape similar to a visual motion sensor. Magda ran to grab her ice-axe and once back, proceeded to smash the shape. Abruptly, the space in front of them began to blink, patterns shimmered, the scenery of the beach had suddenly disappeared. A metal wall of a prefabricated building.

"Hologram," Magda headed to the right, to an armored door with a small numerical keypad. She blew a handful of dryer sand at it and closely observed the most discernable fingerprints. She started pressing the number keys.

"We're at the top," proclaimed Denis once they reached the summit of the hill. He sighed, turned around, with a smile on his face. Kováč had pulled out a gun a moment ago and aimed it at him. "Just as I thought. What about your Butterflies?"

"Don't take it personally, Morar. You're not naive like Sundström, but your team has already outlived its usefulness to me."

"If I was a naive person, I wouldn't have done any background checks on you. I wouldn't have checked to be extra sure. I was expecting this."

"You don't know the code," noted Chae.
"Oh, but I do," smiled Magda. She entered the right combination on the fourth attempt. *Retinal scan*, a voice spoke up from the keypad.
"A small base on an isolated island, in a virgin timeline. Kováč and his henchmen didn't put much effort into a proper password," she explained. She asked Chae for her tablet and spent a while searching in it. "Bhule's team provided me with a high-res photo of Kováč's face. This retinal scanner is a pretty cheap type, you can fool it with a photo of an eye."
Confirmed.
Chae was smiling from ear to ear.
"Crafty gal. Maybe you should lead the team instead of Denis."
Magda pulled the armoured door wide open, laughing.
"Open sesame."
Only the emergency lights illuminated the corridors. There was a similar panel with a keypad next to the door. Magda took her ice-axe and immediately started smashing the panel.
"A precaution. You'll see," she explained to a surprised Chae.

"You simply don't get it, Morar. This is not about me and my subjective impressions, or about my disappointments. You don't see into it on a deeper level."
"You don't say..." Denis calmly replied. It wasn't the first time someone was aiming at him.
"I had the opportunity to study some of the most secret records of the main IDA intelligence taskforce. Some timelines are origin points of threats that would make you afraid to fall asleep, for the rest of your life. Several suspicious alternate Earths have been identified."
"Such as?" Denis asked carefully, but without skepticism.
"TL-8319. Industrially devastated, urbanization unchained. The people from that timeline had decided to resolve the problems at hand… with peculiar measures. These had ultimately failed, and so they used their advanced technology for a quiet, gradual invasion of another timeline, TL-973. Do you now understand why, for a number of years, the IDA didn't recommend traveling to that timeline? Slowly but surely, the lot from 8319 had prepared a breeding ground for carrying out their plan in 973. A plan justified with alibist ideas that had not been subject to constructive criticism for far too long... Until they ossified into outright secular dogma, which only deepened the harm done to their purpose and efficiency. Go on, just ask the citizens of 973, witnesses of the invasion from TL-8319. Ask e.g. Crane, Finch, Knockwood or Gagnon. They'd have stories to tell… Resistance members. The Newcomers from TL-8319 went crazy on their home town, until the locals figured things out and ejected them out of there, with great difficulty."

"Bingo," said Magda. They entered the structure carefully. The interior of the hidden building consisted of only a few corridors, a small storeroom and several smaller work rooms. "The same amateur passwords everywhere, minimal variations. Kováč et al don't have a high opinion of others' intelligence."

Her and Chae entered a smaller laboratory.

"If the IDA had come across all of this, they would have really clipped the butterfly's wings," opined Magda.

"Bert made a good guesstimate. And this is certainly just a small fraction of what they gradually transported to this timeline," said Chae quietly. "An itty-bitty forward base on the island." She walked over to a control panel, tried one of the codes used by Magda. It worked on the second attempt. She felt a gust of cold air.

"Magda, we've probably hit the jackpot!" went her excited exclamation. She carefully pulled out the built-in drawers and, along with Magda, looked at the labels next to each of the stored cryocylinders. "Species from Helena. *Upupa antaios*, *Zapornia astrictocarpus*, the cuckoo *Nannococcyx psix*. As well as species outside the island. *Pinguinus impennis*, *Dusicyon australis*, *Cylindraspis peltastes*, *Epioblasma haysiana*. Hm, *Bos primigenius*..." she paused, contemplating. "I know two people who would be very pleased with this."

"If I understand well," said Denis placidly, "Some group or part of humanity in some timeline had not only botched the environmental situation, but then also botched the effort at correcting the mistakes with an inappropriate approach. And then they gave up on any other solutions and simply decided to grab and colonize some non-devastated timeline. Right?"

"Yes. When I found out about this in copies of documentation from the secret archives, I was becoming outright depressed. I had a real inkling then to write off the entire shitty human race… in every single timeline!"

"But you didn't. You need partners in crime for your little dream colony, for your little utopia. Therefore, paradoxically, you also want to nab a timeline all for yourself. The entirety of this particular virgin Earth."

"We wouldn't even be the first. There was a case years ago, with a certain Baxter investigating a group like our own. Though this is hearsay, in the end, it seems they had even convinced Baxter to join them. I won't be doing the same with you. You and your companions simply know too much."

"Charming. You'll get rid of us for the sake of your personal wannabe-utopia. One established by theft."

"Don't judge me, Denis. You don't have the slightest right to judge me and my companions. None of them, whether they're people from TL-75 or dozens of other timelines, want to continue suffering the oppression of, not so much institutions, as human… human stupidity."

"Then how are you any different compared to that invasion from TL-8319?"

"We're not going to repeat the mistakes of the past and the mistakes of others. And we'll block access."

"No, you're not going to repeat mistakes, you're straight up making new ones," replied Denis with an ironic undertone. "Mr. Kováč, explain to me one more thing: How did you manage to break through so many levels of IDA security? Where did you gain knowl..."

"I'm a naturalized citizen of TL-75. As a matter of fact, I'm originally a native of TL-1. My ancestors had long-term professional relations with high-ranking IDA institutions in TL-1, the main member of the group of IDA-founding timelines. Let's say that my adoptive TL-75 isn't the only one where many people solve various matters… through acquaintances."

"Sure," Denis did a resigned chuckle. He looked around for a possible escape route or for a momentary mistake by Kováč that could provide an opening.

A growing humm and whirr was heard from the south, with a dot in the sky growing ever bigger as it approached.

"My friends are coming," said Kováč.

They heard the buzz of an approaching helicopter. Kováč's collaborators were landing on the beach.

Magda pulled out a pocket periscope, pointed its telescopic head from behind the doorframe, observing the beach. The helicopter was winding down its engine, a team of well-equipped men with automatic weapons exiting the passenger compartment. She put away the periscope, snuck over to Chae and quickly described the situation.

"What do we do?!" Chae whispered nervously. "They'll find us here… Do you have any ideas?"

"Actually... Yes, I have! Come on, briskly to the storage room. Do you remember the active camo we saw lying around there?"

Kováč's men carefully entered the secret structure on the beach. The sight of the apparent burglary unnerved them. They turned on their flashlights and laser targeters, checking every corridor, every room. Magda and Chae were hardly breathing. They kept as close to the walls as possible, slowly sneaking towards the main exit. One team member had just entered the structure, walked past them by only a narrow margin. Now or never. They ran outside and slammed the armored door. Magda lifted her ice-axe and smashed the outside control panel as well. Blocked. Two futile shots, insults and screams were heard from the inside.

"Told you," she raised the ice-axe triumphantly.

"Mr. Kováč, you probably know that I used to live in TL-75 for a while, much like you. In that timeline, they once had a scientist, a popularizer of science, who pointed to a photograph of the Earth taken by a probe from a distant part of the Solar System. The Earth was only a tiny, pale blue dot, only a speck of dust. He had an interesting consideration, a rhetorical question for the audience. Thinking about all power-hungry people, conquerors, tyrants who, in the past, constantly fought over that tiny little dot in the vast universe. All of that just because they wanted to, for a fleeting, mortal moment, become the rulers of a piece of that tiny dot. Pathetic, don't you think? You've reminded me of that, unfortunately enough... "

"You're a pathos-dispensing poor sod, Morar. You're pathetic! And a criminal. Couldn't you find an honest line of work?"

"If you were a self-confident person, Mr. Kováč, you wouldn't be insulting me. You're weak. Only the weak insult, threaten and intimidate. Even those who pretend to be the biggest champs."

"When my bullet punctures your skull, what will it matter!"

"You're weak. You don't have the nerve to do it. And you're not paying attention to your surroundings," Denis said calmly, and made an odd hand gesture.

A tranquilizer dart, fired from Rémy's air rifle, sunk into Kováč's thigh.

Kováč yelled with pain, Denis rushed him, jumping towards his legs. Kováč tried to fend him off with a kick, but groggily stumbled in place. Denis grabbed him by his forearm, pushed his hand with the gun aside, trying to wrestle the pistol away from Kováč.

Kováč was raging, he fired unsuccessfully several times. He almost managed to point the muzzle at Denis' face, but Denis yanked the man's arm upwards, deflecting it. Kováč shoved him, Denis fell awkwardly. Kováč angrily unsheathed his knife and threw it at Denis, who barely dodged it, by an inch. Rémy was running up the hill towards them, shot a few warning shots over Kováč's head.

"Don't move!" he shouted.

Kováč didn't listen, awkwardly fired two rounds. Click. Empty mag.

Angry, he threw the gun away and jumped at Rémy. The submachine gun hit the ground, Rémy fell, quickly scrambled to stand up. He noticed that Kováč had grabbed the handle of the machete on his belt and pulled it out. Rémy grabbed the submachine gun and used it as a shield against the incoming cut. Kováč attempted another cutting strike, but Rémy's counterblow with the SMG knocked the machete out of his hand. However, the SMG had once again fallen out of his grasp, hitting the ground. Kováč grabbed it and ran down the hill.

"Ruddy hell..." hissed Rémy.

Denis ran to him, pistol in hand, helped him get up. They ran down the hill. Along the way, Rémy grabbed the air rifle, pulled a spare pistol magazine for Denis from the backpack, and turned on his walkie-talkie.

"Magda. Chae. Kováč is armed, he's approaching your location. I shot him with a tranquilizer dart, but it's probably too small a dose for a human. Take cover!"

Chae was ready to take off her active camouflage cloak, when Magda waved at her frantically. She had picked up her walkie-talkie just a moment ago.

"Chae, Kováč's shown his true colours! He's nabbed a weapon and is running straight towards us."

Chae-won's expression was genuinely terrified, a chill went down her spine.

"W... what... what now?! Sabotage the helicopter to prevent it from leaving? I... I... I don't know. Magda, dammit! What'll we d..." her nervous calls were interrupted by a pistol thrown through the air. Chae caught the pistol clumsily, looked at it with surprise.

"Magda, you know I'm a geneticist, I'm a pure boffin. I'm no sharpshooter!"

"Necessity is the mother of invention," hurriedly replied Magda. "No time for sabotage. Keep your camo on and hide behind that old log, you'll cover me. Disengage the safety, point and shoot at the guy. Shit, he's coming!"

Chae barely managed to turn on the camo again, when Kováč came rushing from the edge of the forest. During his escape run, he had fallen and gotten bruised. He seemed groggy, but he was still able to stay on his feet and run at jogging speed.

He saw Magda jumping behind a large rock on the beach. He emptied a few rounds in her direction, but she was skillfully hidden. He stopped for a moment, and to his horror, noticed the revealed building with blocked doors. He swore, the roar of the surf dampening his loud obscenities. Him and Magda exchanged several shots from their submachine guns.

Suddenly, he had a hunch of something approaching him, even though he couldn't see it. Abruptly, a thick old branch had appeared in front of him, swung in an arch and slammed him straight in his face and shoulder. He stumbled. Chae had suddenly appeared in front of him, aiming a gun.

"Don't move, you bastard!"

He struck her to the ground with the foregrip of the stolen machine pistol and started running to the helicopter. Chae fired two or three times, but wasn't having much luck aiming properly. Nevertheless, one round had scraped Kováč's calf.

He limped to the helicopter, emptying the magazine while on his way, in an effort to drive away Magda. He threw away the gun, got in, kickstarted the engine. Magda and Chae attempted to approach carefully, but the vehicle was starting to take off.

Denis and Rémy came running out of the forest. Denis impulsively shot at the helicopter, but it was more of a helpless shaking of the fist. Kováč had escaped them.

Magda and Rémy collected the weapons and packed them. Denis walked over to Chae and gave her a tired hug.

"Don't worry about it. You two did what you could," he said, then turned his sight towards the pounding heard from behind the armoured door. "And apparently you caught a few of Kováč's pals. The people working for the IDA will celebrate this catch."

"I was afraid that idiot would shoot me," Chae gave him a tired look. She suddenly became lively. "The animals! What about the animals?! Didn't they get sho..." she asked, but Magda, instead of answering, pulled her active camo tarp from what appeared outwardly as a pile of sand, and smiled benevolently. The storage cases.

Chae finally smiled again after the past stressful minutes.

"I was afraid they're done for," she did a sigh of relief.

"Jolly," Denis turned to the resting teammate. "That dose might not be completely effective, but still has some impact. If it doesn't put him to sleep, there's still a chance he won't be able to concentrate and won't fly all the way to his destination. Right?"

Rémy nodded.

"Okay then. We can no longer influence that. Chae, you and Magda come with me, we'll collect our cartridge casings from the firefight. We'll minimize any evidence we were here. Rémy, how much time do we have?"

The return journey went without a hitch. Rémy wasted no time with reminding them that, were it not for his scent spray marking of the route, finding the way back would've been much harder. However, despite regular rest, they realized they were quickly depleting their time reserve. While they were in the mountainous inland, Denis made a hard decision: They'll release part of the heavier captured animals. Chae wanted to protest, but ultimately agreed. A pair of hoopoes and a pair of rails were already acting lively, and once let out, slowly walked back to the forest. A few hours later, the team descended back into the northern valley and approached the coast. Besides the crashing of waves and chatter of seabirds, they also heard the barks and mellow growls of some sea lions resting in one corner of the rocky beach.

"Boss," said Rémy. "The locator's found something near the portal. An active object, most likely artificial."

Dammit, Denis hissed silently and rushed after his teammate. Rémy reached the spot, it was only a few metres away from the entrance. "Kováč placed some stones there, huh? Just so we don't notice. An amateur after all."

"He didn't even expect I'd find that strange counter-sensor case in his backpack," Rémy said with derision, removing the stones along with Denis. He lifted an egg-shaped metal device with an outside, tubular stand. "A real ostrich egg of doom," he whistled.

"What in the heck is that?" asked Chae, running towards them. "That bastard had deceived us, right? Pebble in the shoe my..."

"Bad. Ruddy! This is bad," Rémy wiped his forehead. "I don't know for sure, but these gizmos are derived from techologies from TL-8319 or 20. When it activates and goes kerblam, it'll deprecate an entire area for any unstable portal creation. Depending on the set range, it could cover every corner of this island. Hard to say. At least we know that Kováč was being serious about his threat."

"Jolly, how much time do we have left?" asked Denis. "Isn't it possible to dispose of it?"

"How exactly? We chuck it into the sea? The detonation would still affect the island. We don't have any experts at hand, so..."

"No portals out, an isolated island in the Atlantic, almost no people in this timeline."

"Yes, Chae. If we don't get rid of it, we'll be done for, but if we lose portal access to the island, then..." Denis was becoming nervous, then suddenly went silent. "Let's try. Rémy, does it have any weaknesses?"

"If you can get a lead case with a lock, a titanium case with a lock, a concrete room with armoured doors and..." he fell silent, a satisfied smile appeared on his face. "I'll call Bhule. The portal will give us a hand."

Magda's face became animated, she apparently understood.

Chae looked uncertain.

"Will we disarm it on the other side?" she asked hesitantly.

Rémy showed her his watch. 4 minutes.

The signal sent from his radio went through the portal, and in a few seconds they received a response. The portal became more pronounced, once again a wavy apparition, like air above a campfire. Denis and Rémy picked up the detonator and entered the portal together. Magda did a quick check-up on the condition of the animals and samples in the backpacks.

"Come on, we have to go," she commanded.

Chae-won nodded, looked around the island one last time. They entered.

Cape Town

"A lead case, with lid and lock! Titanium case, the same, but bigger! Fast!" shouted Denis as soon as they found themselves back in the hall with the secret portal.

Bhule and a few of her co-workers came running, confused. Two of them didn't hesitate and ran to one of the base's secret storage rooms. No one was sure how long the detonator would remain stable. Soon, the portal-handler's colleagues came rushing back, pushing a cargo trolley carrying two heavy cases on top. Rémy didn't hesitate, he immediately placed the "egg" in the lead case, locked it quickly. Then, with the help of Denis and the others, they lifted the lead case and placed it inside the titanium case, then locked that one as well.

A subdued but increasingly loud sound was starting to spread from the locked cases. They didn"t waste any more time, the four strongest people from the team and the staff started pushing the cargo trolley. They arrived at a hastily prepared room with thick concrete walls. They rushed in with the trolley, ran out of the room, slammed and firmly secured the armoured doors. In less than ten seconds, a series of muffled sounds were heard from the room, sounds that were closer to a cross between industrial noise and electric sparking than an explosion. After half a minute, it was all over.

"Command centre and drive room! Damage report!" Nkosazana called nervously.

"Mateusz here," his voice spoke from the intercom. "The portal's functional, energy sources and local networks as well."

Nkosazana breathed a sigh of relief and looked at Rémy and Denis.

"I'll forgive you this time. I warn you, next time, don't get yourselves tricked by saboteurs. Cross-timeline technology isn't exactly cheap," she said seriously. "As for Sundström, trust me. I'll never live it down that he should choose his friends more wisely..." she smiled.

"It wouldn't be a bad bet to let someone in the IDA know about Kováč and his followers in that timeline. You should pull some strings, and in turn, we'll give a tip to Bert. Maybe we'll make 'em happy."

Busan

"Chae, I'm sorry it didn't quite work out with that dou..."

"Oh, shut up, Denis. Let's be glad Kováč didn't fool us completely and we didn't end up badly. Life is more important than a full payment. You told me so yourself. You dabble in these things for other reasons than just mercenary ones. I mean, at least I hope you do."

"You're right. After all, I doubt you'd focus on the research of species genetics if your interest didn't go any deeper than just having a stable place. I wouldn't call it a cushy position."

"Any news on Kováč? Did they catch him, or anyone else from his little conspiracy?"

"Bert didn't disappoint, we provided him with intel to tip off the IDA. They sent a team to that Virgin Earth timeline. They haven't found Kováč yet. Who knows if he survived the escape. They only found his locked henchmen."

Saint Helena

"Stand aside," commanded the Indimpol security team captain.
The furious banging from the inside of the armoured door ceased.

The detonators were activated, the plastic explosives deployed on the outside of the door detonated. The door opened sharply, almost flew out of its hinges despite its mass. From the inside, several vengeful bullets came whizzing past, a few stun grenades and one or two gas grenades were lobbed inside.

The gunfight continued in vain for some twenty seconds, diminishing as it went. An attack command was issued. They ran inside. It was all over in a minute. One badly wounded, two lightly, the others gave up.

"How's it going?" asked Dr. Kwei-Armah, walking towards the captain.

"These goons have been secured. Kováč is nowhere to be seen, he supposedly escaped alone. And they've mentioned an unknown group of four. Your people find anything?"

"Aside from this building, there's nothing man-made on the entire island," he handed a tablet to the captain. "But the technicians came across a minor hint of an anomaly at this spot on the northern coast. It can no longer be tracked, but someone had probably aided Kováč."

"Hm. Thanks. If your team has permission from the higher-ups, you boffins can collect some samples for your own needs."

The doctor returned to his colleagues, the captain was now alone. He looked around, watching his surroundings.

The edge of the coastal groves lay nearby, becoming a thicker forest at the foothills of the valley. The captain noticed a bird sitting on a nearby stunted tree. A Saint Helena cuckoo. Strangely, it was looking directly at his face, with his Inuit features. As if looking straight into his eyes. And *quietly judging*. For a brief moment, he felt a chill down his spine. In a nearby thicket, a flightless pigeon ruffled its feathers, recently disturbed by the noise of the grenades.

Busan

Denis pulled one of the cryocylinders out from the travel bag and held it above the table. "But you've said, aptly, that DNA alone isn't enough to revive a species. Maybe in terms of population, but reviving a species in terms of behaviour, that's far harder," she rolled her eyes in disbelief.

"True. However, do you remember what that Nepalese guy had mentioned? In terms of genetics, yaks are closest to aurochses, especially wild yaks. China in your home timeline is properly democratic and federalized. Perhaps their government could be talked into lending a few yaks from the Tibetan borderlands to Korea?"

"For the animal park?!" she looked at him, befuddled. "You'll have them fertilized in vitro, carried to term by surrogate females, and then the dad and mom yaks will raise the first aurochses in more than half a millennium?" she sniggered.

"It's worth a try. Korea has a mild climate, very similar to central Europe. First they'd grow up, learn their main survival instincts, then we'd move them to central Europe, let them run around in reserves alongside wisents. And so on, and so on, until they reach a more genetically stable population. Eventually, maybe even export some of them to other timelines."

"There are no doubt government programs as well."

"Perhaps. You don't hear much about them," he leaned a little closer to the table, and continued more quietly. "And no, this is not purely about fulfilling my old dream. I had several of the cryocylinders donated to that guy who was sad about the government limiting any efforts to revive the aurochs species in his timeline."

"Oh, my!" her voice rang with gentle irony. "Denis Morar, so generous, all of a sudden. You're getting older, you're becoming a softie. Just keep it up, and you'll become a modern day Robin Hood, or what. But you're not going to rope me into another smuggling date, no siree," she concluded and drank some tea.

"We'll see," he shrugged and grinned modestly.

TL-2004

The interior of a spacious tree hollow. A large hoopoe peered inside, then entered. The female was looking after the eggs, with one of them already hatching. The male looked at the hatching egg, noticing a baby hoopoe slowly breaking free and climbing out of it. The parents raised their feathery crests and did a signature "upupoo" sound, seemingly happy.

The old-growth tree with the hollow stood on the large property belonging to Sundström.

Saint Helena

Another family of hoopoes was resting in a more exotic-looking cloud forest of a lush, mountainous island. They did an "upupoo" vocalization as well, as if calling upon their relatives in another timeline.

The Virgin Earth version of the island of Saint Helena was encircled by the waters of the Atlantic, on all sides. Waves crashing against the coast, calm blue waters as far as the eye could see...

Peter Molnár

Peter Molnár is a kid of the late 1980s and 1990s and a native of the Zemplín region in east Slovakia. He works full-time as a professional translator of fiction and non-fiction, focusing on bilingual English language translation. (Among other things, he was the first to translate a book by John Howe into Slovak.) In his free time, he focuses on reading, chess, hiking, cycling, sightseeing, amateur archery and bushcraft, creating small documentary videos, as well as writing speculative fiction and various other fiction. He also occassionally works on designing tabletop gaming and freeware computer game projects, all based on his own intellectual property and fiction.

The Battle of Maldon

Joshua Boers

The Battle of Maldon took place on 11 August 991 AD near Maldon beside the River Blackwater in Essex, England, during the reign of Æthelred the Unready. Earl Byrhtnoth and his thegns led the English against a Viking invasion. The battle ended in an Anglo-Saxon defeat. After the battle Archbishop Sigeric of Canterbury and the aldermen of the south-western provinces advised King Æthelred to buy off the Vikings rather than continue the armed struggle. The result was a payment of Danegeld of 10,000 Roman pounds (3,300 kg) of silver (approx £1.8M at 2022 prices). An account of the battle, embellished with many speeches attributed to the warriors and with other details, is related in an Old English poem which is usually named The Battle of Maldon.

Because the poem is in Old English (Anglo-Saxon) there are several different translations, all of which address the meaning in the text, but choose different word forms due to emphasis, or context.

Here, Joshua Boers had undertaken a unique project, to take the original Old English text of a verse, and rearrange the letters into a Modern English rendering of the same.

Lines 309–319, anagrammed line by line into Modern English

Byrhtwold maþelode, bord hafenode	=	Deft bard-hero howled bloody anthem.
(se wæs eald geneat), æsc acwehte;	=	(We see death's ace wag a steel cane,
he ful baldlice beornas lærde:	=	bane's elder fuel heroic ballad!)
"Hige sceal þe heardra, heorte þe cenre,	=	He: "Learn thee rage, re-ice the chest-hoard!
mod sceal þe mare, þe ure mægen lytlað.	=	Man's death rattle helm thy melee-courage!
Her lið ure ealdor eall forheawen,	=	Oh, here lieth our fallen war-leader,
god on greote. A mæg gnornian	=	a good man gone. Gain no regret
se ðe nu fram þis wigplegan wendan þenceð.	=	unhewn gent, fleeing this death-strewn camp. Ha!"
Ic eom frod feores; fram ic ne wille,	=	scoffed warrior. "Me, I'll ice foemen!
ac ic me be healfe minum hlaforde,	=	Maul me, each blade, for mine chief!
be swa leofan men, licgan þence."	=	Fence! Lance! Men lose with a bang!"

Devil's Dyke

Susan Dean

I didn't like the house when I first saw it, I felt sorry for it that first time in the auctioneers photographs on their website. Dejected, dilapidated unloved probably for decades, yes what Erica, my wife had found was just the sort of property we had spent many hours discussing and had finally decided was what as a family we wanted. We had made a unanimous decision that the cash made from selling my parents house and the not unsubstantial inheritance left to Erica by a distant relative if combined would enable us to purchase a rundown property to convert into luxury period apartments. Martin, our son had his own construction company and would undertake the necessary work involved he viewed it as a great advertisement for his business and was already looking at extending into period restoration work. This was to be a side line for us a safety net if you like in the unpredictable world of employment something to fall back on if times got tough.

Erica found the house a Victorian mansion on an auction website and instantly fell in love with it but I had misgivings, not that I wanted to do a U-turn on our agreement it wasn't that it was just that house even in the photographs there was something I felt wasn't quite right. But Erica was sold on the property 'We might get it at a snip if we play our cards right, it needs quite a bit of work but we might just get it a really low price' she wheedled 'Victorian at a guess' I asked moving closer to get a look over her shoulder 'mmm' she agreed. Throughout the morning Erica persisted with her persuasive wheedling 'why' I asked for the hundredth time 'that particular property' 'I don't really know' she confessed 'it just feels like it's calling to me, oh come on, we have a free afternoon ahead of us we could just take a look' she whined. 'OK' I sighed 'you win after lunch we'll drive over and take a look at the place Devil's Dyke isn't it' I queried 'yes' she replied smiling triumphantly 'shouldn't take too long to drive over it's about half an hour from here.'

By mid-afternoon we were parked on the grass verge outside the rusting but decorative wrought iron gates 'typical Victorian' I hissed under my breath. Erica shot me a warning look 'what' I asked 'you know how I hate all that heavy Victorian stuff' 'I know' she laughed and pushed open the partially open gate whose rusted hinges groaned in protest and we walked up the tree lined drive to the flight of stone steps gradually becoming hidden under a profusion of weeds and up to the double front doors which were padlocked. 'Not very sociable are they' I quipped 'very funny' Erica sarcastically retorted 'let's take a look around the back' she suggested already beginning to retrace her steps heading around the side of the house with me quickly following.

We had to fight our way through the encroaching brambles the sound of broken glass crunching under foot, moving all manner of rotting debris littering the ground as we made our way. Some of windows were broken their filthy net curtains escaping with the aid of the wind, although we were able to peer inside through one or two of the dirt streaked panes which revealed several rooms of varying sizes. All of which were still furnished one or two items had had sheets thrown over them as had been the custom when leaving a home for some time. Particles of dust danced among the beams of what sunlight could manage to penetrate the dirt of time reflecting the blues, reds and yellows of the stained glass patterns. 'Looks like they left in a hurry' I remarked 'and never returned' added Erica 'I wonder why' she mused. Through an open interior door we glimpsed a heavily ornate oak staircase and even one or two of those enormous potted plants the Victorians were so fond of dead of course. 'Odd place' I remarked voicing my thoughts 'let's take a look around the grounds' 'OK' agreed Erica. As we moved away from the house further into the grounds Erica suddenly shivered and looked back 'are you OK' I asked the day was warm but the grounds were so overgrown that much of it was shaded and cool. 'Yes' she replied tilting her head to look up at the upper floors 'what's the matter' I asked 'seen a ghost' 'I'm not sure I just had a strange feeling we were being watched that's all' 'seriously' I almost laughed but seeing how pale she was decided to stifle it 'Come on let's take a look around.'

Although overgrown the original layout of the various gardens were still discernible but the tangle of foliage made for a great deal of shade which caused the paths to be frequently lichen covered making them damp and slippery. Dead roses hung their heads sorrowfully from their branches along with decayed rhododendrons, honeysuckle was rampant and one or two statues needed a cleaning and repairing while a fountain needed a clearing out along with the stagnant pool surrounding it. But the walled kitchen gardens were largely intact even greenhouses had survived well the entire property had that feeling of having just been left as if the owners had been in a great hurry to leave but as to why mystified us.

'Well, what do you think' I asked turning to Erica as we made our way back to the car 'call Martin see what he thinks and we'll make a decision this evening' 'OK sounds good to me' I agreed reaching into my pocket for my phone.

Three weeks later we had put in a bid and been accepted much to our surprise the house or rather mansion at Devil's Dyke was now ours. Once we had the keys we drove over while the grandchildren were at school taking Martin and his wife, Sheila with us principally for a look at how much work was needed and how we were going to turn it into luxury apartments.

Opening the front door for the first time in decades its sheer size took our breath away the silence felt oppressive as if lying heavy on the stale air and there was a smell of luxuriant decay. Dust covered everything even gas lamps were still adorning the walls with oil lamps on some surfaces 'no light switches' noted Martin 'the place doesn't even have electricity, wow' he exclaimed the house was a time piece it even felt like a living, breathing relic. Portraits and taxidermy decorated the walls adding to an uneasy feeling of being watched Sheila broke the silence 'do you think any of the people in these portraits lived here' her voice echoing around the dim space 'who knows' answered Martin 'but let's see what the rest of the place has in store for us.' We moved through the house from room to room finally ascending a narrower flight of stairs taking us to the top floor which had once been servants quarters and obviously storage rooms then Erica opened a door at the far end of the corridor and gave a gasp of surprise. 'A nursery' she called out her voice shattering the eerie silence that pervaded the upper floor 'did you have to shout so loud' I whispered 'sorry, why are you whispering?' queried Erica although her own tone was noticeably lower 'it just seems more appropriate somehow' I replied as the four of us stepped into the room.

A child's bed lay across one wall still made up with the original linens as far as we could tell that is, a nursing chair stood near the window with a collection of both china dolls and those with heads made from wax which gave them that sickly yellow look arranged on the seat their eyes seemed to be staring at us, a cold calculating shade of blue which made us feel as if they were following our every move. I shuddered and looked away only to find myself staring into the grinning face of a wooden rocking horse the gaping maw displaying a set of enormous teeth which reminded me of tomb stones its seemingly lifeless glass eyes glared back at me. An assortment of tin soldiers had been thrown haphazardly into a tin box on the window sill and a variety of soft toys were arranged on a shelf beneath that was a large trunk. A set of drawers and a wardrobe completed the nursery furnishings both women shuddered 'let's get out of here' Erica said voicing what we were all thinking 'those dolls make me feel uncomfortable it feels like they are watching us' 'Yes' agreed Sheila 'those things are going to be among the first to go, ugh.' The dolls heads turned to watch the the door close as they left the room but I felt sure I heard the rocking horse move to and fro as we left although I brushed that aside telling myself that was just letting imagination run away with me. But despite that the old nursery had left us feeling unnerved and we couldn't get out of the house and back to the car quick enough.

The nursery they had left behind unbeknown to them had returned to life after so many years of lying dormant. Lucinda the largest porcelain doll in the collection slowly rose from her place on the nursing chair and carefully climbed down one of the chair legs and strode purposefully into the centre of the room steadily rotating her head around the toys and with a steely glare spoke with an air of menace 'so we're going to be among the first things to be got rid of are we they'll soon discover that we're not things. I think it's time we had a little fun again are we agreed?' The toys all turned to look from one to the other sickly grins spreading across their faces and nodded in agreement.

Sheila had volunteered to start the cleaning up process in readiness for work to begin on the renovation but decided on starting on the Saturday as Eleanor, their eldest daughter being keen to see the house, had offered to help her mother so a none school day was picked for work to begin.

By mid-morning on the Saturday Sheila's car pulled into the drive at Devil's Dyke and began unloading cleaning materials from the boot entering the house by a rear door which opened into a dark narrow corridor a kitchen was on their left 'servant's entrance right' remarked Eleanor dumping buckets, scrubbing brushes and refuse bags in the kitchen 'well, yes you could say that but wait until you see what's at the other end of the corridor' 'what' she asked intrigued 'hang on a minute and you'll see, you can help me carry all those dead plants outside from there for a start' 'Oh, Ok then' she replied peering round the kitchen doorway trying to see what lay ahead. 'Right then' her mother said a few minutes later wiping her hands on a towel 'follow me'. She followed her mother further along the corridor and after a few seconds noticed it was getting lighter then she suddenly gasped in surprise. The corridor suddenly opened into a winter garden a kind of atrium the room was large supported by ornately carved pillars, the floor was beautifully tiled but littered with dead leaves dust and dirt there were several sofas and one or two arm chairs in the corners and enormous decaying pot plants that once towered above the furnishings reaching for the light now drooped, brown and dry as stone. But its most attractive feature was the high glass domed ceiling 'wow' gasped Eleanor tilting her head right back to look at the ceiling 'this is really something I love it' Sheila merely smiled and said 'right come on let's get these plants outside.'

It was while Sheila was getting their packed lunch from the car that Eleanor alone in the winter garden finishing sweeping up the last of the debris suddenly shivered and looked about her unable to shake off the feeling that she was not alone. She turned quickly when she thought she saw a movement from the corner of her eye, a shadow perhaps *but whose shadow* she thought and there it was again on the opposite side of the room she was sure of it 'hello, who's there?' she called out but only the oppressive brooding silence of the house greeted her and that was something she hadn't noticed before how silent the house was. The shadow if that was what she had seen seemed to move towards the open French window and vanished into the garden impulsively she ran after it.

Outside Eleanor ran first down one path and then another twisting and turning until she became confused searching for a figure she couldn't be certain she'd seen. The afternoon was growing darker then the first rumble of thunder boomed quickly followed the first drops of a heavy downpour. Eleanor spotted a gazebo and ran towards it almost falling up the steps in her haste to shelter from the rain and sat down on a stone seat supporting her upper body with her hands placed on the seat either side of her torso then crossed her legs at the ankles and began to absent-mindedly swing them to and fro. What felt like an eternity passed as she sat listening to the rain beating down on the gazebo roof water leaked in from above and dripped from leaves. She shivered from the fact that it had inexplicably turned so cold that she could even see her breath on the air. Then she froze a small ice cold hand was creeping over the back of her left hand she could feel the tiny fingers begin to curl around her own, she swallowed hard took a deep breath and forced herself to look round, at first she saw nothing but a dim view of the dripping wet garden then a violent flash of lightening light up the interior of the gazebo just as she lowered her eyes and there sitting beside her staring up with large sad doleful eyes was a young child. Eleanor swallowed then in a barely audible whisper stammered 'who are you?' the child simply looked up at her 'don't you have a name?' the child remained mute but looked towards the house then back at her. In blind panic she leapt up from the seat and fled down the steps oblivious of the rain and just ran. Dimly aware of her mother's voice calling 'Eleanor, Eleanor where are you' then with a sudden crash she ran straight into her mother almost knocking her off her feet 'Eleanor where have you been? what made you go out into the garden in a thunderstorm?.' She began sobbing 'I thought I saw someone a child I think' 'You must have imagined it there's no one here except the two of us. Come on let's go home and have lunch there you'll feel better when you've eaten and I have the school run to. How about you come with me?' She nodded and they headed off.

During the week Erica helped Sheila start taking down curtains while Martin boarded up the broken windows and by the following weekend she decided she felt a little better about her previous weeks experience and returned on the Saturday with her mother. She was busy packing the old curtains into bags and boxes when she thought she felt a chill in the air *must be a draft somewhere* she thought and carried on working, then she stopped and listened as she thought she heard a voice she shook her head and returned to the packing. No there it was again a low whispering that was becoming louder she was sure of it a low coaxing voice 'Eleanor' the voice tempted 'we're lonely come and play with us' she shuddered and tried to ignore the voice but there it was again 'Eleanor we've no one to play with come and join us' with no knowledge of the nursery she turned towards the stairs and began walking towards them. 'That's right' the voice wheedled 'come and play' just as she placed a foot on the first step her mother shouted 'Eleanor come and give me a hand will you' the voice instantly vanished the spell broken.

With the following week being half term Eleanor spent more time helping her mother the house now had running water again and she was in the kitchen making tea using the old range even the clothes airers still hung from the ceiling. Sheila was outside sorting out what rubbish was next to be taken away when a bell rang Eleanor was so surprised she almost dropped the kettle she was holding and went to see where it was coming from. She stared in disbelief at the push bell board each bell had a small brass plaque under it engraved with the name of the room under each one the bell that was ringing said 'nursery' she blinked in disbelief who on earth was in the nursery she hadn't even known there was one let alone it's location. She walked into the winter garden looking around her then covered her ears as bells all over the house started to ring simultaneously the jangling sound was almost unbearable in the normally silent house. The French doors flew open and there stood the child she had seen two weeks earlier she was terrified she wanted to run but her legs wouldn't move then the child beckoned her and vanished into the garden. Instinctively she knew the child wanted her to follow and reluctantly moved forward. Once outside she saw the child waiting for her beneath the overhanging branches of a tree and again beckoned she continued to follow until she came to the fountain there the child stopped slipped her icy hand into hers and pointed to the pool then looked back towards the house before beginning to vanish again. She had the feeling the child meant no harm but was trying to tell her something she knew then that she had to find out whatever she could about the house and the family that had lived there whoever they had been.

Shaken by this new incident by the time she reached the house and found her mother she had decided that she would start with the local library and told her mother that she was taking the next day off to do some studying. 'Studying' her mother asked looking surprised 'it's half term and you have studying to do you didn't say anything before about having school work to do.' 'I know mum I just forgot I'll come back with you at the weekend Ok?' 'Of course' her mother replied 'you don't have to come with me at all if you don't want to' 'I know mum.'

With Erica busy the following day Sheila decided to take a radio over to the house with her as the brooding silence was beginning to feel increasingly menacing and she hated the thought of being entirely alone with it and Eleanor's behaviour was worrying her she felt that something wasn't right and she felt sure that whatever it was was connected to the house. She stopped off to buy batteries for the radio on her way over to the house muttering to herself about being glad when the old place finally had electricity and drove off.

When she arrived at the house the first thing she did was put the batteries in the radio, tune to a pop station and leave it playing in the kitchen. The sound seemed to cut through the silence like a knife through butter but she was glad of the company it made her feel a little more comfortable but not enough to stop her look around nervously as she left the kitchen the feeling of not being alone never seemed to leave her.

She headed for the stairs intending to begin rolling up the old carpet ready for removal and was about half way up when the feeling of being watched suddenly began to intensify she turned her head around and screamed. Watching her through the balusters were three toys only they looked nothing like innocent toys the first a Pierrot doll was staring down at her it's stark white chalked painted face filled with hate, it's cold blue eyes glared down at her filled with an evil madness a sickly grin crossed it's hard cruel wooden mouth it's wooden fingers curled around the carved spindles. Next to the doll sat a stuffed rabbit it's torn right ear hanging limp over its right eye, a worn teddy bear stood next to the rabbit she stared in horror at the toys then noticed the jacket the bear wore had dark stains on it old but they did look like blood. Recovering her wits she ran up the stairs snatched up the toys exclaiming aloud 'who left you lot there horrible things' and ran clutching the toys up to the nursery kicked the door open and flung them into the trunk slamming the lid shut 'there, you all belong either in a bin or a museum – ugh hideous things I hate the lot of you' then slamming the door shut stormed back down the stairs.

'Well you heard her' came a voice from inside the trunk 'let's teach her a lesson it'll be fun' Lucinda got up from her place on the nursing chair and slowly climbed down the leg pausing only to look around the room at the toys then focused all her attention on the door handle concentrating hard summoning all the power she could until the door knob slowly began to turn and the door swung open.

Downstairs with the radio playing Sheila heard nothing as Lucinda made her way down to the ground level stairs and stood on the landing watching Sheila work. By now the carpet had been taken up and it surprised her to hear a ball roll down the stairs making a soft sound as it slowly bounced from one step to the next she turned at the unexpected sound catching a brief glimpse of something on the landing as the ball rolled past her. Looking up she saw a porcelain doll standing there glaring at her with murderous intent. She let out a final scream of sheer terror as the doll slowly began walking down the stairs towards her never taking its cold calculating gaze away from her. In both surprise and terror Sheila made to step back lost her footing and fell down the stairs then lay still on the cold tiled floor of the winter garden in a hideous twisted heap. Unable to move her terrified eyes could only watch the doll's slow determined advance. Then it knelt beside her unable to move her twisted broken body and incapable of responding to her brains natural responses to save herself. She could only watch as the doll leaned over her placed its small porcelain hands over her windpipe and begin to apply pressure she squeezed harder and harder until Sheila could no longer fight for breath and the final spasms of life finally left her. Lucinda stood up looked down satisfied with the deed she had done turned and walked back up the stairs to the nursery.

Once out of sight an apparition appeared, a small child looked down at the pitiful sight of Sheila's broken crumpled body lifeless eyes staring up at the glass domed ceiling. A small hand turned the screw on a gas lamp, the hiss of fuel barely discernable, then the child approached the tools left by the construction workers and turned on the blow torch. There was a whooshing sound as the flame found the gas; the figure vanished as the house went up in flames sending Devil's Dyke into oblivion.

Alea Abiecerat – Park 6

Haley Receveur

Recap

    History in the world of "Alea Abiecerat," which is a rough Latin of "The die has been thrown away," is identical to the history of our world up until January 10, 49 BCE. Gaius Julius Caesar was elected consul, led a successful military campaign in Gaul (approximately modern-day France in our world), then saw the Senate threaten his political future. Seeking power and immunity from prosecution, Caesar in our world led his troops across the Rubicon River into Roman Italy, effectively declaring war on the Republic. In our world, he made his way safely to the other bank and successfully defeated his opponents, Gnaeus Pompeius Magnus (more famously known as Pompey) chief amongst them. Caesar became a dictator and was famously assassinated by the Senate. His nephew, who would later become known as Augustus Caesar, then carefully laid the groundwork to transform the dead Republic into an Empire which would come to dominate the Mediterranean, shaping the history of our world for centuries thereafter.

    In the alternate world of this story though, Julius Caesar suffered a tragic accident. His horse panicked in the crossing and, with a well-placed kick, snapped the general's neck. The would-be dictator died in the middle of the river, dragged back to shore by his soldiers. Mark Antony, Caesar's ally, takes the opportunity to boost his own political standing and takes charge of Caesar's troops, now leaderless. A majority of these troops followed Antony across the river, hoping for payment, while a small portion retreated back to Gaul. Antony began to move throughout Roman Italy, pacifying city after city, either by force or generosity.

    Antony's movements and troop consolidation panicked the Senate, which quickly authorized Pompey to lead a force against this insurrection. As Antony marched through Italy, with more violence committed against his enemies than Caesar did in our world, Pompey established a camp in the fields outside Rome, hoping to prevent Antony's army from entering the city.

    The vengeance-minded Antony, fresh off executing Lucius Domitius Ahenobarbus (great-great-grandfather of our world's Emperor Nero), made his way to the great city. Both Antony's and Pompey's forces mercilessly fought each other for the soul of the Republic. Somehow in the chaos, Pompey took a spear to the chest and died. His less-tested and less-motivated troops scattered, leading Antony's battle-forged soldiers to win the day and take the city.

    Opposition senators fled Antony's advance and began making their way to other territories. Some found themselves in Sicily but most headed for Sardinia, hoping to use the island as a base from which to consolidate power and attack Antony when the time was right. In elections in August of 49 BCE, Marcus Porcius Cato Uticensis (better known as Cato) and Marcus Tullius Cicero became the consuls on the island, standing in firm opposition to Antony's activities on the mainland.

Meanwhile Antony moved swiftly to consolidate power. Fancying himself a true "man of the people," Antony worked to endear himself to the plebeian majority, promising grain and prosperity. He led a high-profile march to the treasury and threw open its doors, in effect bribing the impoverished masses for their support. In consulate elections in Rome that year, Antony and his handpicked partner Publius Cornelius Dolabella were easily swept into office. Though Antony was often politically at odds with his co-consul, he recognized that Dolabella would be useful in endearing Antony to the patrician class. This sometimes tense alliance enabled Antony to further consolidate power in Rome.

But Dolabella was not as strong an ally as Antony had hoped. Dolabella used his position to subtly undermine the young upstart and push Antony into sometimes reckless action. This was especially true when it came to Rome's foreign entanglements. Antony's first concern was to stomp out the rebellion brewing in Sardinia, thanks to the escaped opposition. Dolabella, however, was able to assuage Antony's ego enough to assure him that his reign was secure and that his attention was needed elsewhere. This prevented bloodier civil conflict between Romans while helping to secure Rome's borders during this chaotic period.

The most consequential of these foreign entanglements was the brewing conflict in Egypt between King Ptolemy XIII and his sister Cleopatra. In general, this put Roman troops right on the border of the Egyptian kingdom, ready to take up arms in support of one of the two parties should such an eventuality become necessary, and was simply an issue of national security. Dolabella manipulated things such that Antony's allies would be in charge of this portion of the Roman army and thus not part of the equation in Roman Italy. Antony was all too willing to give his allies patronage.

However, though Dolabella was astute in manipulating Antony, he could not foresee the threat looming in the north of the dying Republic. Titus Labienus, who in Caesar's absence found himself the leader of the Roman legions stationed in Gaul, declared Mark Antony's government illegitimate and threatened war. There was increasing talk in the camps of Labienus that the general will declare himself a king, take Gaul for himself, and threaten Roman superiority on the continent, but at the time Antony heard of this declaration this talk had yet to translate to meaningful action.

The Roman world of 48 BCE stood on a precipice. Antony and Dolabella held together a sometimes-tense alliance to continue to project Roman power on the world stage. Many powder kegs were lit across the known world though and threatened to explode: Cato and Cicero could mount a retaliatory attack any day; either Ptolemy or Cleopatra could make a false move in their squabbles and drag Rome into the conflict; and, from the barbaric north, Labienus could sweep down and put an end to Antony's career. It remains to be seen just how these threats will be managed and if Antony's regime will survive the ensuing chaos.

Part 6

Potheinos strode along the banks of the Nile River, flanked by royal guards. The floodwaters were beginning to recede, and Potheinos could see farmers tilling their crops on the far bank while fishing boats leisurely sailed down the swollen river, casting their nets to ensnare the plentiful fish. The boy king, now at the tender age of fourteen, had been crowned just three short years prior. Potheinos, a eunuch who had faithfully served the Ptolemaic court for years, was the boy's regent until he came fully of age.

It had not been a smooth reign, to be sure. Though Ptolemy's father's will had stipulated that the boy and his sister, Cleopatra, marry and rule the kingdom jointly, the foolish girl had gotten in her head that she was the rightful ruler. She had attempted to style herself as a pharaoh of old, learning Egyptian like the common folk and donating much of her wealth to support traditional cults to the ancient pantheon. The girl had cast off her Greek ancestry, an act which would surely invoke the wrath of the first Ptolemy upon the royal house. To make matters worse, the insolent girl had effectively usurped her brother's throne. She had taken to styling herself as the sole ruler of Egypt, denying her brother what was rightfully his. Potheinos had grown fond of the boy king, or at least he had grown fond of his newfound political power. He could not abide such a breach of tradition and decorum.

Ever since Cleopatra's ascent, Potheinos had plotted her downfall. Recently Ptolemy had succeeded in wresting power back from his sister. He was now signing documents with his name first before his sister's, taking his rightful place as the head of the co-monarchy. Nevertheless, Cleopatra and her forces persisted in causing trouble for the young king. Cultists and military forces loyal to her continued to do battle with Ptolemy's own loyal forces. General Achillas, who commanded the king's troops, almost daily told of these struggles. Often he was triumphant against the traitorous queen's cabal, but any loss was too much for Potheinos. Any loss threatened to destabilize Ptolemy's legitimacy. Any loss threatened to cripple the boy king's resolve. And any loss threatened to bring Potheinos' head one step closer to a pike. No, Cleopatra's continued attacks on her brother's reign would not do.

"I asked if you thought this was a fine harvest, Potheinos," Ptolemy said, snapping his boyhood tutor-turned-regent out of his thoughts. Ptolemy had spent the walk with eyes on the river, surveying his domain and secretly hoping to see a crocodile.

"Yes, your majesty. The gods smile on us this season." Potheinos stopped in his tracks and, bowing his head, turned to face the king. "Forgive me, sir, I am afraid I was lost in thought."

Ptolemy too stopped walking and turned to face the wizened man. "Lost in what sort of thought?" He paused for a moment then suddenly realized what was troubling his mentor. "Is it what General Achillas spoke of this morning?"

"Very astute, my king," Potheinos said, straightening himself and continuing to walk. Ptolemy sidled up alongside him and turned his head to face his taller companion as he listened to the eunuch vent about Cleopatra's attacks.

"Nevertheless, Potheinos," Ptolemy said in a stern voice, turning his head forward and continuing to walk, "she is my sister. She may be a nuisance, but she is still of royal blood."

"Of course, your grace, forgive me," Potheinos said, hoping he sounded apologetic. "I did not intend any insult. I merely want what is best for your kingdom and your reign. Have you given any more thought to your other sister? Arsinoë?"

Ptolemy walked along in silence for a moment, then stopped and stared back out at the river. "This river truly is a marvel, Potheinos. From some unknown point in the middle of nowhere many hundreds, if not thousands, of stadia away, this mighty river flows into the sea, supplying our kingdom with a bounty unheard of throughout the known world. This river was here for thousands of years, and was impossibly ancient before the first of my dynasty was conceived. And it will be here thousands of years after I pass into the afterlife, after my squabbles with Cleopatra are but whispers in the dunes."

"I know it well, your majesty," Potheinos said, coming to stand beside the king. "I used to play along its banks as a child, before I was blessed to serve your family. In that time, I have seen the river rise and fall for countless harvests, some better than others. In some years, the river swelled peacefully, providing those who depended on its waters with all the bounty they needed. In other years though, the river swelled uncontrollably, devastating the crops and sweeping houses out to sea with its monstrous currents. The river is mighty, my king, but our ancestors refused to simply bow to its whims. We erected dams with the express purpose of telling the river exactly how it should flood."

Potheinos turned towards the king and placed a hand gingerly on the king's shoulder. He still remembered the day the king came into the world, a squalling babe with no inkling of the destiny which lay before him. Over the years, Potheinos had taught the boy history, science, mathematics, Greek, Latin, and philosophy, all in the hopes that the boy would someday be ready to take his father's place amongst the line of kings of this storied kingdom. Looking at the boy now, Potheinos wondered if he had failed in his duties to instruct the young king. He was much too naive and much less aggressive than his father. The late Ptolemy XII would have put down this rebellion the moment it began. He would not have shown his own sister mercy. For the good of the kingdom, the former Ptolemy would have done what was right. But this younger Ptolemy was not as keenly aware of the dangers Cleopatra posed to his reign. He did not see the dissent her actions were making plain. He did not see that her rebellion and insubordination would lead to his downfall.

"Do you remember my lessons, your majesty?"

"My friend, I scarcely remember what we ate at last week's feast."

Potheinos chuckled politely, though he was slightly annoyed at the king's dismissive attitude. "History is like a river. It flows on and on without beginning or end. We just simply step into its stream for awhile, but upon our death the river continues to flow as if we had never stepped foot in its cooling waters at all. Many are at the mercy of time's river. Those farmers across the bank have no way to influence the river's flow. They cannot hope to construct a dam in their lifetimes powerful enough to alter destiny."

Potheinos let go of the king's shoulder, staring down at the young Ptolemy and hoping he understood his former tutor's meaning.

"But my father," Ptolemy said, realization clearly dawning, "he wished Cleopatra and I to rule together, to marry. Rome herself was supposed to guarantee it."

"Rome," Potheinos said with a snort. "They are in no better state than we are. Most of their senators have fled to a tiny island across the sea. Pompeius, their most capable politician, lies dead, killed in some vain quest for a swift resolution to Marcus Antonius' crusade. And I am told that Antonius himself, who took up arms to rule the city and her people, has fled into the wilderness in an ill-conceived effort to silence one of his own rebellious generals. No, your majesty, Rome is in no position to guarantee anything." He stood in silence for a moment, looking out across the horizon. "You still have not told me what you think of Arsinoë."

"Well, she is certainly prettier than my other sister. She was also always more compliant when we were children. And she certainly respects my father's traditions more than Cleopatra does." Ptolemy turned his head back to the palace then, shaking his head, stared back at his mentor. "Your council has not yet turned me astray. I will propose marriage to Arsinoë. Together we will rule this kingdom and bring it the stability it deserves."

"A wise choice, my king," Potheinos said, turning to look at the young man. "You will make a fine ruler, and I very much look forward to providing you guidance for years to come, even long after I am your regent."

"Does Achillas have a plan?" Ptolemy said, putting an abrupt end to what Potheinos hoped would be a solemn moment between teacher and student.

"Yes, your grace, though I think it best if you do not know of it in exact detail. No need to concern yourself with such…messy affairs of state." Out of the corner of his eye, Potheinos spied a small boat sailing towards him. *Just in time*, he thought. "I must take my leave now, your majesty. Gentlemen, please escort our esteemed king back to the palace. He has a wedding to plan."

Reluctantly, Ptolemy strode away with his guards. Potheinos stayed on the riverbank and reached into a small purse he had concealed underneath his robe. Fiddling with the straps, his fingers brushed against a small glass vial, filled to the brim with a clear bubbling liquid. He lifted it from the purse and palmed it, waving hello to the fisherman he had paid handsomely to discreetly deliver the rebel queen's gift.

Haley Receveur

Haley Receveur is a budding alternate history writer, based out of Indiana. She graduated with a bachelor's degree in history from the University of Louisville, and with a master's degree in public history from IUPUI. Her main historical interest lies in the late-nineteenth and early-twentieth centuries, but she has a background in ancient Roman history from her years studying Latin. She is fascinated by the political intricacies of the late Roman Republic and feels that the era presents a gold mine of alternate history possibilities. Alea Abiecerat is a serialized story, continuing to go forward.

Immortality Bites!

Glenis Moore

Most people think that immortality might be great, at least for a while, but I can tell you that it is nothing like it appears in 'Highlander' or even Doctor Who for that matter. In fact it certainly has its downsides as I have discovered over the years.

The first time I died, at nineteen in a motorbike accident, it was fantastic to wake up in a cosy hospital bed with all of these people around me asking me how I was feeing. It was a bit confusing at first, as they kept calling me Charlotte, when I was sure my name was Anne, but I wasn't about to complain seeing as how I thought that I had died. I found out later that I had been 'transferred' into Charlotte and was now living her life so I had to learn a whole new set of relatives, friends etc but, despite the fact that I never got everything right, they all put Charlotte's oddity down to brain injury in the accident.

The second time I died I drowned (not something I would recommend to anyone by the way) and woke up on a beach being given the kiss of life by a portly Japanese man. It transpired that I was now a 39 year old Japanese house wife called Yushiko. Again I had to learn a new set of rules quickly but I was always a fast learner so no problems there.

And so it went on, but I soon cottoned on to the fact that every time that I died I came back as someone of the same age so I was gradually getting older. This did not seem too good as it meant that I would probably spend the fag end of eternity as an ancient crone getting slowly weaker and weaker but never actually dying. So when I died as Maria in a small Peruvian village at the ripe old age of one hundred and fifteen I was not looking forward to waking up again.

I did though and was almost frightened out of my immortality as this time I found myself in a pod like thing surrounded by large purple creatures with lots of teeth! I thought, this is it then – Hell – but they seemed very friendly and, despite the obvious species difference, I seemed to know what they were saying.

They were the Astasii from a planet somewhere near Andromeda, I think, but as one hundred and fifteen is really young for them I didn't know too much and was still at school. I could manage their language without any issues but their food looked pretty disgusting, to begin with, and alive. However, as I have Astasii taste buds I soon got used to it despite the need to catch it first.

I felt relieved. Other species have longer lives so I could go on being Astasii for another four hundred years at least and then who knows what I might become. Until that is I found out that their plans were to invade Earth and eat all of the inhabitants, who were considered a gourmet speciality ever since they had found an astronaut floating around and lost from a space mission I had never even heard of – you don't hear much about space missions in the Peruvian Andes.

What was I to do? After all I had lived my first one hundred and fifteen years as a human and most of them did not seem that bad and certainly not edible. I thought about it for a while and then came to a momentous decision. I was only an Astassi child so they wouldn't listen to me so what was the point complaining or trying to make a case for the survival of humanity. Humanity hadn't thought too hard about destroying other creatures on their own planet so why shouldn't they go the way of the Dodo etc.

Anyway tomorrow we're off. They say that it won't take us too long to get there in Astassi years and then it'll be time for lunch. So maybe you should all think carefully next time before you kill an animal as one day soon you may be predated as well by us flying purple people eaters!

Glenis Moore

Glenis has been writing since the beginning of the first Covid lockdown as it seemed like a much better idea than taking up baking. She does most of her writing at night as she suffers from severe insomnia, and when she is not writing fiction, she writes poetry, makes beaded jewellery, reads, cycles and sometimes runs 10K races slowly. She lives in the flat lands of the Fens with three cats and her long-suffering partner Nick.

On Creating Aqua and Uni

Lily-Isabella Logan

Lily-Isabella Logan had the idea for AQUA AND UNI since she was in Grade 3 as a game she used to play with a friend. Over the years, Bella worked on the story with her stepmother to transform what started as a homemade paperback into the imaginative friendship fantasy story it is today. Lily-Isabella lives in Toronto, Canada with her family, a feisty cat and an adorably rambunctious dog.

She writes:-

"In grade 3, around Halloween, we had an assignment where we had to make a scary story. My teacher showed us how to fold paper in a way that looked like a book. My best friend at the time and I made one together, but during that time we played a game where I was a half-mermaid, half-human named Aqua and my friend was a half-unicorn, half-human named Uni who had to run away from the evil Queen of Peas and her family. We then decided to make the story of the *Aqua and Uni* into a book, using the paper folding technique. What started with just the two of us soon became more as we got more friends to be other characters to join in the game. After about a year, we finished *The Adventures of Aqua and Uni*, a story that takes place 10 years after Aqua and Uni go to camp. My best friend and I lost touch since we were different in classes and COVID-19 happened. That's when my stepmom and I decided to write a prequel to the original story. After many years of brainstorming, writing, editing and trying to get published, we finally did back in May of 2023."

These pictures are of Bella with the paper fold-out book

Aqua and Uni Go To Camp was published by Dancing Unicorn, an imprint of Purple Unicorn Media, on 14th May 2023 with the following blurb:-

Aqua and Uni Go To Camp is a story about friendship that takes place in a magical summer camp. We meet Aqua, a half-human, half-mermaid orphan, and Uni, a half-human, half-unicorn princess. We follow Aqua and Uni as they attend Camp Fairy-Tale, meet the children of other fairy-tale characters, have new adventures, and solve the mystery behind a camp curse that threatens to uproot everyone's summer fun.

The book can be purchased in paperback or Kindle on Amazon, and in epub ebook format on a range of platforms including Barnes and Noble for Nook, Apple iBooks, Kobo and Scribd.

Paperback ISBN 978-1915692283

https://www.amazon.com/dp/1915692288

Where Imagination Can Take Us

Sue Woolley

I am a simple soul at heart. When I read a book, I like to know whom I'm supposed to be rooting for. Which is why I love reading fantasy so much.

Having grown up with an early partiality for myths and legends, the graduation to reading fantasy was a natural one. My first contact with a proper, grown-up fantasy came at the age of 13, when I read J.R.R. Tolkien's *The Lord of the Rings* for the first time. I was on a long coach trip to Germany with the school and, being entirely unable to sleep in a moving vehicle, just read and read and read. This was like nothing I had ever encountered before – I had never been so completely involved in a story. I became totally absorbed in the world of Middle-Earth and felt a shock as keen as pain when I reached the last sentence: "'Well, I'm back', he said."

Since then I must have read *The Lord of the Rings* well over a hundred times, and always there is something new to notice, something enchanting to savour. I had never come across an author who realised his fictional world so completely – history, geography, different peoples and their customs, mythology – it is all there.

So perhaps it was inevitable that I would one day want to try my hand at writing a fantasy of my own. And I knew that the "worldbuilding" would be enormous fun, so I spent many hours working out all the details of my fantasy world, the Commonweal of Veylindré. I even drew a detailed map, of which I am ridiculously proud.

I knew from reading books by many authors of fantasy that the task of bringing such a complicated world to life would be easier if I could hang the events of the plot onto some kind of underlying structure. In the case of *The Stones of Veylindré*, I decided to use the twelve-point structure of the Hero's (or in this case, the Heroine's) Journey, which is used by many fantasy writers. But I also wanted to explore how the beliefs we hold and the choices we make have can have a really significant impact on our lives.

I also knew that I wanted my main character to be from our world, so I made her a seventeen-year old girl from England in the 1660s, Abigail. She leaves England with a small group of pilgrims and during a terrific storm in the Atlantic, the pilgrims are translated to the Commonweal of Veylindré. When the rest are murdered by pirates, Abigail vows to make a new life for herself in this strange world, with her boyfriend, Jacob. Some Dagâran people befriend them, and Abigail and Jacob soon realise that Veylindré is quite different to the England they left behind. All Veylindréans worship the Six, and are able to do magic by accessing the mysterious Way through their Goldstones. But they have an enemy, the Prophet of the One, who rules in Talamdor. The choices Abigail and Jacob make in response to the changes they experience have huge consequences for both their lives…. If you want to know any more, you'll have to buy the book!

It took more than three years to write the first draft of *The Stones of Veylindré,* and 18 months more to revise it, before I sent it out to beta readers. More revision followed, and it was not until March 2022, that I began to approach publishers. And was delighted when Scimitar Edge, a small, independent press, agreed to publish the first volume, *The Goldstones and the Way.* Which was published in mid-November and is now available through Amazon. The second and third volumes, *The Prophet and the Wayzenmoot* and *The Bloodstone of Talamu,* will be published next year.

Available in paperback, Kindle, and other ebook formats

http://www.scimitaredge.com/the-goldstones-and-the-way.html

Book Review – Atomic Secrets

By John A. Hopkins

In some ways this book is in the tradition of Len Deighton's "SS-GB" or C.J. Sansom's "Dominion", though in another way it has more in common with Robert Harris's "Fatherland". But whilst you can create these comparisons, the global political structure in "Atomic Secrets" falls into a different category. Britain is not defeated, but Nazi Germany remains. Quite how this has worked out is not obvious, but the world we are in is the important part. More data and information comes along as you read the story.

Obviously, as the name of the book suggests, it is the race to create a viable atomic bomb which is the centre-piece of the novel, and this is hardly a spoiler. The USA, Britain, and Germany all have projects of their own, but the German project has only now to come to light, being brought to the attention of British Intelligence by a potential defector within the Third Reich.

The main character, such as there is one, is David Brooks, the man chosen by the British to be inserted into Germany to stop the atomic project, a fact that should be no great give-away of the plot. In this, he is ably supported by the Welshman Jamison, at the Board of Trade within Dresden. What the author does really well, from hereon in is keep what characters know what separate, which takes some skill.

The supporting cast, in what could be a movie set in the old East Germany, where the Stasi would take the role of the Nazis, are exceptionally well-drawn, from the haughty SS Brigadefuhrer Mangold, to the cast of police offiers from the Kripo, including the amusing (to English ears) ranked Kriminalrat Behrend. There are a couple of strong, and prominent women characters – the scientist Koenig, and the police investigator Sabine Saller.

This is not quite the Nazi Germany of Hitler, or indeed of Goering, as Heydrich is now Fuhrer, a very sensible choice by the author as the menace and danger of the Nazi regime is well-maintained, with the threat of the Gestapo ever in the background.

The plot proceeds along several parallel threads, and some necessary info-drops are made when characters have to tell other characters, who were not present on certain occasions, what they have found out, or what is going on. This is natural to the plot, useful to the reader, and does not feel forced at all.

Mention must be made of youthful womaniser, Wilhelm Daluege, the most junior of the cast of Kripo, but possibly the most insightful. His sub-plot, driven by his ability to join things together adds the immediate drama of the second half of the book.

There is some beautiful detail along the way, such as in the cast of cars, from an Allard to a Horch and a BMW, to a small DKW, and to the rarer Stoewer.

You might say there are two canvases, that of Britain at the start and that of Germany, for most of the book. Of the two, the latter is the most compelling, and is grittily drawn, from dodgy block masters, to homeless veterans, warehouses in rundown areas, and yet an opera and smart cafes at another instance.

Whilst the colour might be said to be brown and grey, there are lots of different shades to these colours, and eventually the story takes off into greener pastures.

Altogether, a very enjoyable, tense story, excellently cast in a fascinating setting. Atomic Secrets comes highly recommended.

https://www.amazon.co.uk/Atomic-Secrets-John-Hopkins-ebook/dp/B0CBHGPGJN/

Book Review – Cold Rising

By Rohan O'Duill

This book was an unexpected treat. I had vague Bladerunner meets Total Recall thoughts from the blurb and description, before I started, but the novel forged its own path and one was soon immersed in the author's own unique world.

In some ways the novel is a clash of cultures within this world, twice over. On the one hand, we have the agents in the dark corners of an Earth town, doing their thing, then meeting their corporate bosses, in sky-touching towers of luxury. On the other hand, we have these agents themselves as fish out of water, sent to Mars, and running into the unique culture that is there, on the ground.

Olgo is the lead agent in the story, a gender neutral individual with a traumatic childhood which they shut out with emotional blockers. They are effective, intelligent, but morally ambiguous. Their team includes the psychotic Stevie and the hulking man of muscle, Glebe.

This team we get to know on their first, Earth mission, then we follow them to Mars, where their story intersects with the second parallel tale in this book, that of Suong.

This 12 year old girl's life is a mixture of what we might think epitomises the worst of contemporary Chinese industry and of Victorian attitudes, but it is far better than it could be. As long as things go well, she has a job, a home of sorts, a family, and a study period. She can dream of more.

But things do not go well, and we find ourself at the time of the blurb, Olgo cast into the darkness, and that little voice, of Suong's, calling out to them...

I found this book a fantastically enjoyable read, that really sucked me into the worlds of the author's imagination, soon coming to care about the characters and experiencing their emotional journey towards its conclusion.

Cold Rising can be purchased on Amazon at:

https://www.amazon.com/COLD-RISING-Cold-Rush-Novella-ebook/dp/B0C97RVRMT

Uncle Rollo's Railway

By Mark Carter

Rowland Bates and his wife buy an old railway station which has been converted into a modern house.

Bates, a steam train enthusiast, discovers that the railway line is still there, partly buried beneath the long grass and brambles, and with the help of three local children who call him 'Uncle Rollo', he uncovers the track so that it can be seen again, running past the 'station'.

They discover a rusty old guards van and an ancient steam engine, long abandoned, in a derelict corner of the property.

Bates takes on a retired engine driver, Edward Bere, or 'Teddy', to help get the engine going. He also discovers the railway line continues, still partly buried, across his neighbour's land, and seeks permission to uncover the track over there, too.

With the help of the three children, some friends and Teddy Bere, their gala day arrives with the opening of UNCLE ROLLO'S RAILWAY.

https://www.amazon.co.uk/Uncle-Rollos-Railway-Mark-Carter/dp/1915692458/

A Road So Travelled by Brian G. Davies

A Road So Travelled is an entrancing mixture of autobiography and travel articles, fully illustrated with photographs, and covering 9 decades of the 20th and 21st centuries. This autobiographical book includes the authors memoirs of his childhood as an evacuee with family in South Wales, and later boarding at King's School, Ely, and many travel articles from later life, including to Singapore, across Canada in a motorhome convoy, a coach tour of Italy from top to toe, a visit to Turkey, including the site of Troy, taking the Pilgrim Route to Compostela, and visiting Eastern Germany.

https://www.amazon.co.uk/dp/191071819X

Brian Gwilym Davies, formerly of Knighton, Powys, lately residing in Swansea, passed away at Morriston Hospital, Swansea on Wednesday 19th January 2022 aged 88 years. Beloved husband of the late Maureen, loving Dad to Jon and Beth, devoted Grandad to Imogen, Bryony and Ceridwen, loving brother of Colin. His funeral service took place on Wednesday 9th February 2022 at 11am at Knighton Methodist Chapel, with burial at Knighton New Cemetery.

Donations in his memory to Cancer Research UK remain welcome.

Purple Unicorn Media Catalogue for 2023

Purple Unicorn Media
2023 Catalogue

Purple Unicorn Media & its registered imprints
GREY WOLF

PUM Catalogue 2023

Lists all books in print or in preparation across the 3 imprints of Purple Unicorn Media, Scimitar Edge, and Dancing Unicorn, as well as the magazine Infinity Wanderers and associated titles, self-published under the Selornia marque.

£5

https://www.amazon.co.uk/dp/B0C1J9Z5HX

Back On Track by John Kennedy

The cover for Back On Track was designed by Joe Swarctz

Back on Track is a story about an Irish Catholic family arriving in Youngstown Ohio from County Tipperary in 1845 who met both Triumph and Tragedy. Resuscitation arrived five decades later when third generation great grandson John Kennedy embarked upon self employment founding a Railroad Construction Co in the state Capitol in nearby Pennsylvania.

But a second resuscitation arrived on October 10, 1988 when the author got and stayed sober, salvaged a company, and provided a roadmap for his family to follow that has made all the difference in getting where life can be lived with peace and purpose not squandered.

https://www.amazon.com/dp/1915692326

A Few Wild Beasts To Be Dreaded by Ralph Greco, Jr.

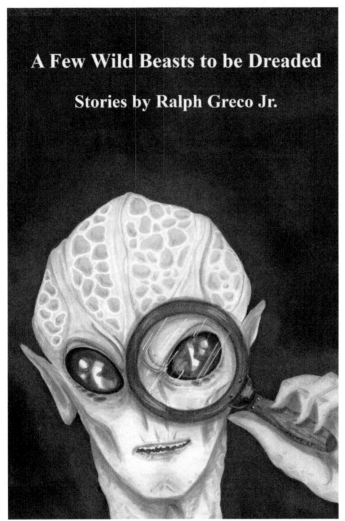

The cover for A Few Wild Beasts to be Dreaded was created by Joe Swarctz

This mixing of the fantastic with the satirical, the sexy, and just the downright odd (or even all 3 in one story) is at the heart of this fiction collection, A Few Wild Beasts To Be Dreaded.

https://www.amazon.com/dp/1915692083

Aqua and Uni Go To Camp by Lily-Isabella Logan

Aqua and Uni Go To Camp

Aqua and Uni Go To Camp is a story about friendship that takes place in a magical summer camp. We meet Aqua, a half-human, half-mermaid orphan, and Uni, a half-human, half-unicorn princess. We follow Aqua and Uni as they attend Camp Fairy-Tale, meet the children of other fairy-tale characters, have new adventures, and solve the mystery behind a camp curse that threatens to uproot everyone's summer fun.

https://www.amazon.com/dp/1915692288

Sophocles – Three Plays

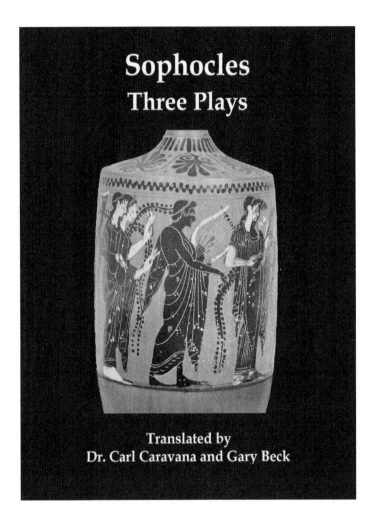

Dr. Carl Caravana, an excellent Greek scholar, worked with me in a process that functioned well for us. Dr. Caravana started with a literal translation of Electra. We examined the nature of the characters, the poetic elements of the text and we did another version. Once we were satisfied that we sufficiently maintained the integrity of the original I concentrated on finalizing the text for stage production. We followed the same process with Antigone, with a little more focus on the characters who were the victims of fate, the main theme of the play.

The Searching Satyrs, The Ichneutae, only existed as a fragmentary satyr play, with less than half surviving in bigger or smaller sections. We used the same work process as in the other plays, except I wrote all the missing lines, trying my best to keep them consistent with the original lines. Any mistakes are mine, not Dr. Caravana's.

https://www.amazon.com/dp/B0CJ3X9BZ7

The Wooden Box: And Other Stories

Michael J. Lowis

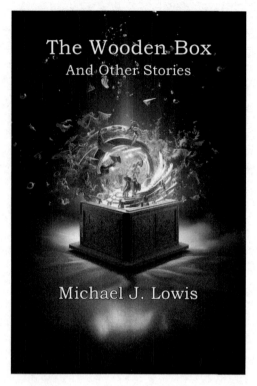

Cover design: Steven Phillips

A collection of short stories of varying lengths and genre, totalling approximately 65,000 words. There is something here for all tastes including mystery, sci-fi, fantasy, crime, memoir, anecdote, romance, and factual discussion.

The mystery of what is in that wooden box kicks off this eclectic collection of 24 short stories, and a topical update on a Christmas Carol concludes it. In between these are tales of adventure, science fiction, mystery, crime and romance. But non-fiction topics are also featured, some based on the personal experience of the writer. Examples include a swapping game, customers enjoying afternoon tea, and what you would save first if your house was on fire. Other stories were inspired by unusual items from the author's cabinet of curiosities, such as a crystal skull, an Aborigine sketch of a god, or water claimed to bring everlasting life. Indeed, there is something here for everyone, and the author's aim is to leave the reader thinking 'Hmm, I wonder if that could really happen.'

https://www.amazon.co.uk/Wooden-Box-Other-Stories/dp/B0CKB3PZXL

Printed in Great Britain
by Amazon

33587463R00117